A King Production

Superstar

Joy King

This novel is a work of fiction. Any references to real people, events, establishments, or locales are intended only to give the fiction a sense of reality and authenticity. Other names, characters, and incidents occurring in the work are either the product of the author's imagination or are used fictitiously, as those fictionalized events and incidents that involve real persons. Any character that happens to share the name of a person who is an acquaintance of the author, past or present, is purely coincidental and is in no way intended to be an actual account involving that person.

ISBN 13: 978-0-975-58114-8
ISBN 10: 0-975-58114-7
Cover concept by Joy King & www.MarionDesigns.com
Cover layout and graphic design by www.MarionDesigns.com
Typesetting: Linda Williams
Editor: Dolly Lopez & Linda Williams

Library of Congress Cataloging-in-Publication Data;
King, Joy

Superstar: a novel/by Joy King
For complete Library of Congress Copyright info visit;
www.joykingonline.com

A King Production
P.O. Box 912, Collierville, TN 38027

A King Production and the above portrayal log are trademarks of A King Production LLC

This Book is Dedicated To My:

Family, Readers and Supporters.
I LOVE you guys so much. Please believe that!!

Acknowledgements

I got so many emails from readers screaming on me for how I ended *Hooker to Housewife*. I've had so much on my plate but I was DETERMINED to give readers the ending they deserved. I love all of the characters in this series, although they are scandalous in their own way. I'm keeping my fingers crossed that I did them justice with my latest installment, because I'm truly grateful for the love, support and patience readers show me. I hope to continue to write books that you all enjoy. Hugs and Kisses!!

I did want to take time to acknowledge a few readers who I feel ride for me extra hard, and words can't describe how much that means to me. For the ones I forgot to mention, I apologize and I'll get you on the next book ☺

Tureko "Virgo" Straughter, Tazzyt2bossye, Ms KiKi, Andrea Denise, Sunshine716, Ms. Monalisa, Lady Scorpio, Travis Williams, Myra Green, Leona Romich, Sexy Xanyell and Linda Williams who is so special you must be an angel. Also, to vendors, and distributors like Black & Nobel, DC Bookman, Tiah, African World Books, Horizon Books, Vanessa Calvin; I love you honey, Afriqiah Books, Maxwell Taylor, Cyrus Webb, Rahman Muhammad, all the book clubs who support me, and every vendor in Brooklyn, Queens, and 125th Street that pass out my bookmarks...thank you!!

Special thanks to Jonesy of Hot 97, you always show me so much love...you're the BEST!! Keith Saunders of Marion Designs, Tracy Taylor, and Darren Coleman, I don't know what I would do without you—you truly are my rock. Larry Satterwhite—thanks for believing in me and being patient. Lastly, my parents Suzy Hoard and Ellery King...I love you both so much.

Much Love,

Joy King

Most importantly, to my readers, I know I left you hanging with *Hooker to Housewife* but I hope *Superstar* was worth the wait—Enjoy!! Please hit me up and share your thoughts. jk@joykingonline.com

Superstar

Chapter One

Beautiful Disaster

Whoever said it never rains in Southern California was mistaken. When it rains it pours, and tonight it was a full blown storm. You could barely hear the loud noises coming from the ambulance and police sirens due to the combination of blistering winds echoing with the thunder and lightening.

Instead of neighbors and passersby finding refugee in their homes or cars, they were fixated by the visuals that resembled images straight from a movie scene: A woman standing with her hands cuffed behind her back wearing what seemed to have been a beautiful dress. The gorgeous face masqueraded by makeup now smudged from the falling teardrops. As the officer read her rights she was too enthralled with the man holding the hands of the woman she had just hit with her silver Benz. It was reminiscent of Clara Harris except there was a psycho bride in a wedding dress behind the wheel. And instead of the intended victim being on his deathbed, the other woman was suffering for his mistake.

"I'm so sorry," Andre said choking back tears. "This is all my fault, baby. Please don't die!" he begged to an unconscious Tyler. He was in shock that the love of his life was slipping away. She was slowly dying and there was nothing he could do about it.

Chantal gazed from a short distance as Andre stepped into the ambulance with Tyler. "Would you please let me go?" she snapped at the police officer as she pushed her body forward. "My husband is leaving and I need to be with him."

The police officers looked at each other peculiarly as if acknowledging they were dealing with a quack. "Lady, the only place you're going is jail. Now please follow me," the officer said as he escorted Chantal to the car.

"Or the Looney bin," the other officer added, slightly laughing.

"Jail! You sound stupid," she barked. "I'm Chantal Jackson, the wife of Andre Jackson. I'm sure you've heard of him. He will not be pleased with your manhandling. Now get your hands off of me!" Those were the last words the officers heard before slamming the car door in Chantal's face.

The drive to the hospital seemed to be the longest ride of Andre's life. After they rushed Tyler in for emergency surgery he went into the hospital chapel and prayed. He felt he had no right to beg for God's mercy, but Tyler shouldn't have to suffer for his sins. First Chantal, and now Tyler was clinging to life, but Tyler was so innocent in all of this. He was the one who had drove Chantal to the edge of insanity, and now Tyler was the one fighting to live. He was positive their baby she was carrying didn't survive, but if she pulled through then they could try for another one. Andre was determined to have a family and future with Tyler. He just hoped that she was just as determined.

When Andre finished pouring his heart out to the Lord he walked back to the waiting room to see if there was any word on Tyler's prognosis. As soon as he stepped through the door every eye was on him. He could hear the news reporter from the television giving an elaborate breakdown of the evening's tragic events. The loud whispers said it all.

"Is that him? Is that Andre Jackson, the man who left his fiancée at the altar and got that poor actress hit by a car?" he heard one heavyset woman whisper to the man sitting beside her.

"Mr. Jackson, can I speak to you for a moment?" the doctor asked, answering everyone's questions. Andre was somewhat relieved that the doctor showed up and he could escape the intensity in the room. They stepped in the hallway and he felt bubbles in his stomach as the doctor spoke. "Tyler suffered serious internal injuries and she's in critical but stable condition. The next twenty-four hours are crucial. If she's able to survive then a full recovery is likely."

"Thank you, doctor," Andre said, not wanting to breakdown. "Can I see her?"

"She just got out of surgery and they're moving her to intensive care. I'll let you know when you can see her."

Andre felt numb. He knew if Tyler died then his life would be over with. His mind was so clouded with sorrow he almost didn't hear his cell phone ringing. He didn't recognize the number but still opted to take the call. "Hello."

"Andre, it's me, Shari. What the hell happened? I'm hearing all these crazy reports on the radio that your fiancée hit Tyler Blake with a car and she's in the hospital. I know they're not talking about Chantal."

Shari was talking so fast he had to take a second to digest her question before answering. "Yes, they are. Chantal outdid herself this time," Andre said calmly.

"What! I don't understand. There must be some mistake," Shari belted out, sounding confused.

"There is no mistake, Shari. Chantal tried to run me over and Tyler pushed me out the way. She's barely hanging on to her life because she tried to save mine."

Andre took a deep breath as he had a quick flashback to the incident. One minute he was holding Tyler, gazing into her eyes and stroking her hair. Then next he was walking to the car and heard Tyler screaming for him to move. But the astonishment of seeing Chantal speeding towards him with her weapon left him motionless. If Tyler hadn't pushed him out the way he would've definitely been rolled over and splattered across the ground. But after the impact of the car sent Tyler flying 20 feet, Andre wished it had been him that was hit. "I'm sorry what did you say, Shari?" he said after finally realizing she had asked him about five questions, none of which he answered.

"Where is, Chantal?"

"I would suspect jail, Shari. That's what they do to people who commit crimes and get caught."

"Listen, Andre, I know you're a little pissed right now."

"*Little?* That's an understatement!" Andre trilled.

"Okay a lot, and I do understand. But Andre, Chantal is the mother of your child and your fiancée, until you left her standing at the altar and had one of your cronies break the news that you wouldn't be showing up now or never."

Shari's attempt to make Andre feel guilty was actually working even under the circumstances. He knew a lot of this was his fault. Chantal proved she was unstable after slitting her wrists when he told her he planned to marry Tyler. But after things didn't initially work out with Tyler he took Chantal back knowing he wasn't in love with her. He locked himself down to a farce of a wedding with the complete knowledge that his heart belonged to another woman. He dragged Chantal along by a string until she reached her breaking point. Now she was in jail and Tyler was in the hospital. He felt like shit.

"What do you want me to do, Shari? Chantal tried to kill me and ended up hitting the woman that I love."

"It's always about you, Andre. You are so fucking selfish. While you sit there licking your wounds I'm going to figure out a way to get Chantal out of jail. I'm sure you all's daughter is concerned about her mother." Shari slammed the phone leaving Andre to wonder how he became the villain in all of this.

The commotion of the paparazzi, a belligerent woman and hospital security woke Andre. He fell in a deep sleep while holding vigil at Tyler's bedside. He looked at his timepiece and it was now eleven o'clock in the morning. Tyler still wasn't conscious, but when she did come too he didn't want her surrounded by chaos.

"What the hell is going on?" Andre asked the bodyguard he hired to stand watch in front of Tyler's room.

The paparazzi immediately started flashing their cameras and shooting off a million questions. "Andre, over here!" one familiar looking television reporter screamed while walking towards him and jamming a mike in his face. "How is Tyler? Is she going to live?"

"Get that mike outta my face!" he spit as the bodyguard shoved the camera crew out the way. "How in the hell did all this press make it to ICU?" a frustrated Andre asked the nurse.

"I don't know, Mr. Jackson. The police have been called and security is trying to control the situation until they arrive."

"Well, they need to step it up. This is outrageous. And who is that woman arguing with Tyler's doctor?" Andre inquired, thinking to himself that she had a familiarity to her.

"I'm not sure. She got here about fifteen minutes ago and has been yelling at the doctor ever since."

"Excuse me," he said heading towards the irate woman and the visually shaken doctor. "Pardon me. Is there some sort of problem?"

The woman gave him a defiant stare that made Andre feel like he was five years old. "Who are you and why are you interrupting me?" she snapped.

"I'm, Andre Jackson, and who are you?"

"Don't question me, young man. You're the reason my daughter is lying in that hospital bed barely alive. You should be ashamed of yourself."

Andre's heart dropped when the woman said "daughter". Tyler only mentioned her mother on a few rare occasions. Once, when she was getting married for the fifth time and the others when she talked about how beautiful her mother was, which she was. Her silky smooth walnut colored skin was adorned by delicate features, which were further highlighted by her chin-length golden-brown bob cut. In her tapered two-piece skirt suit it was evident that she had a dedicated workout plan given the muscle tone on her five-foot six-inch tall frame. But through all that beauty, Andre was at a loss for words as her icy eyes sent chills down his spine.

"Excuse me, I need to check on Tyler," the doctor said, realizing this was a chance for a clean getaway. Andre couldn't blame him, her stare alone was vicious.

"I'm so sorry, Mrs. Blake," Andre finally mustered enough courage to say.

"I haven't been Mrs. Blake in over twenty years. That's Tyler's biological daddy's last name. It's the only thing he gave her that was worth keeping. My name is Maria Chambers, but that's Mrs. Chambers to you." Andre couldn't believe that someone as sweet as Tyler had a mother that literally spit fire when she spoke. "Also," she added putting her hand in the stop position.

"Don't insult my grief with some pathetic sorry. Your sorry ass is the root of all my daughter's problems."

Before Andre could defend himself the nurse ran out of Tyler's room saying that she was awake. He was relieved that security had gotten rid of all the press. Both he and Maria ran towards the room simultaneously as if in a race to the finish line. The bodyguard put his hands up blocking Maria's path. "If you don't get out of my way, you overgrown GI Joe!" she belted.

"She's okay, this is Tyler's mother," Andre said, regretting he defended the woman. Before they could get any further, the doctor was the next stumbling block.

"Tyler, can only have one visitor at a time," he said before catching a glimpse of the determined mother figure. "She's very weak, so please don't excite her and keep the duration of your visit as short as possible."

Maria abruptly pushed past the doctor making way to Tyler. "Oh, Tyler, I'm so glad you're finally up," Maria said as she stroked Tyler's hand.

"Hi, Mother." Tyler's voice was barely audible.

"Oh, honey, I'm so sorry this happened to you. But Mother is here now and I'll take care of you." Maria carefully did a close examination of her daughter before saying, "Oh, baby, thank goodness your face is still beautiful. You only have a couple of minor scratches that will heal in no time."

Andre stood to the side for a minute, trying to take in the piece of work of a mother Tyler had. "Where's Andre?" he heard Tyler whisper.

"I'm right here, baby." Maria gave him the screw face as he approached the bed. "Tyler, God heard my prayers. If you didn't make it, I couldn't have survived without you." Tears rolled down Andre's face as he held on to Tyler's hand on bended knee.

"I'm so glad you're alright. I'm still groggy and I only remember bits and pieces of what happened," Tyler said.

"Well, from what I understand, dear, your boy toy here sent his fiancée over the edge and she tried to run you over with her car."

"No disrespect, Mrs. Chambers, but I don't think this is the time to talk about what happened. Tyler needs to get some rest," he said, wanting to bitch-slap the woman.

"Andre, don't leave. Mother, can you give us a few minutes please?"

"Sure. I'll be waiting outside." When Tyler heard the door shut she collected enough strength to give Andre an endearing smile. "Don't pay attention to my mother. Her bark is louder than her bite."

"You sure about that? She seems awfully treacherous to me."

"I'm sure. Don't let her scare you away."

"From you, never. I'm not leaving your side until you come home with me. Tyler, I was so scared. I know this is all my fault, I hope you forgive me."

"Stop it. This isn't your fault. Chantal is the one who hit me, not you. So stop blaming yourself. I need for you to be strong for both of us, because right now my mind and body are so weak."

"Don't worry, you're my angel. I'll take care of you, I promise." The guilt slowly began to lift off of Andre's shoulders as he lovingly gazed into Tyler's eyes. Even with the scratches on her face and the bandages wrapped around her head he still thought she was the most beautiful woman in the world.

"Baby, I'm really tired. I want to go back to sleep and you need to go home and get some rest."

"Okay, but I'll be back later on," he said before kissing Tyler on her forehead.

"Do me one little favor before you go."

"Anything."

"Tell my mother to come in. I want to talk to her before I go to sleep."

"Anything but that," he said seriously.

"Pleeeeeeease," Tyler begged.

"Only because I love you, but there's a bodyguard right outside your door if you need for her to be escorted out."

"Andre, stop it. She's my mother."

Andre left the room to locate the mother from hell. He didn't have to go far, since Maria was impatiently standing against the wall, tapping her pumps on the floor. She didn't even wait for him to invite her in. She briskly walked past Andre straight into Tyler's room.

"That's some mother Ms. Blake has," the burly bodyguard said. He took the words right out of Andre's mouth.

The moment after closing Tyler's hospital door, Maria let her thoughts be known. "Tyler, I wish I could take you home with me right now. Your doctor is incompetent and these nurses look and act like they belong at some sort of city facility."

"Mother, please. I'm alive aren't I?"

"No thanks to that friend of yours, Andre Jackson. He has some nerve being here when he's the one responsible for your predicament."

"Stop! Andre and I are in love."

"Tyler, Tyler, Tyler. When are you going to learn how to choose your men? You would've thought after that psycho high school boyfriend of yours, Trey blew out his brains, you would use more caution. And let's not forget Brian, my poor grandson's unstable father, now Andre Jackson. You can do so much better, dear. If you continue on this path I'm afraid next I'll be making your funeral arrangements."

"How can you say such a thing?" Tyler said, mortified by her mother's prediction of death.

"Now calm down, you're still weak. I'm not trying to upset you. I'm simply stating the obvious. You go from one dysfunctional relationship to the other. You could've been killed yesterday and that is every parent's worst nightmare. You have a baby to think about."

Those words stung the most. The little brother or sister her son Christian would've had was gone. There was no way she could still be pregnant after taking a hit like that. Tyler figured Andre or did the doctor probably mention it because they didn't want to cause her more grief.

"Mother, can you please go? I'm exhausted. I really need to get some rest."

"But we're not finished," Maria said.

"Yes, you are. I'm going to have to ask you to leave. Your daughter needs to get some rest," the doctor stated as he entered the room.

"Fine, but I'll be back later. You get some sleep, honey."

Tyler closed her eyes yearning for the day her and Andre would make love again.

Chapter Two

Someone Watching Over Me

It had been a little over a month and Tyler was finally going home. With great resistance from her mother, Andre rented a beach house in Malibu. He didn't want her returning to his home and having to relive that horrible night, and due to the enormous press coverage the paparazzi were stalking out her place 24/7. Although Tyler had basically made a full recovery, Andre hired a live-in nurse just in case anything went wrong. He was determined to make sure she had everything she needed. So much had happened in the last few weeks and he didn't want to bring Tyler any more unnecessary stress.

Chantal managed to obtain a top notch LA criminal attorney who had bail set. Somehow she was able to post the money for the million dollar cash bail, and it was rumored from reliable sources that Chantal planned to plead insanity.

Although a restraining order was issued and she wasn't allowed in the same vicinity as Andre or Tyler, she was still free as a bird and walking the streets. The worse part was that his daughter, Melanie was caught in the middle. Every time Andre would see Melanie, she would ask him why he wasn't with Mommy, and why didn't they get married. Or why Mommy was crying all the time. It was overwhelming, especially since he was supposed to be the prosecution's star witness.

Tyler was going to testify, but she didn't have a clear memory of the events that transpired that evening. They were counting on Andre's testimony to put the nail in Chantal's coffin. Andre knew that would destroy Melanie and she might never forgive him. Even though Melanie was too young to understand exactly what was going on, he knew that Chantal, her family and friends would make sure Melanie knew that it was Daddy that put Mommy behind bars. That was weighing heavy on his heart and mind.

Chantal took a long shower so she could think about the meeting she had with her attorney in a couple of hours. Never did Chantal imagine she would be facing 25 years to life for attempted murder. This was her worst nightmare, losing her freedom and her daughter. That was exactly what would happen if she got convicted of the crime. She was determined not to let that happen.

After lathering her entire body with La Mer, Chantal pulled her shoulder-length honey-blond hair up in a loose ponytail. She dabbed a bronzer on her face to bring it life and applied Chanel Berry Cherry lip-gloss, then headed towards the closet to pick out something to wear. She chose her Marc Jacobs cream slick fitting pencil skirt with a waist-length tapered tweed blazer. Her Louis Vuitton leather ankle-strap pumps and monogram canvas soft briefcase were the finishing touch. Chantal might have felt like a wreck but she surly didn't look it. When she strutted out of her subleased apartment in Beverly Hills, she put her best foot forward, determined to win the battle of her life.

"Andre, I'm so happy to be home. I know this isn't a permanent residence but it's a whole lot better than that dreadful hospital."

"It can be permanent if you like. Did you check out the view of the beach?" Andre said as he opened the white silk drapes from the vast windows, exposing the breathtaking coastline and whitewater.

"Yeah, it is definitely inviting. I could stay here with you for the rest of my life. But in reality it isn't that simple. Honestly, I'm feeling a little overwhelmed regarding this case. I'm so tired of this scrutiny from the media. I wish this would all go away. They're actually portraying Chantal as a victim. What is this world coming to?"

"I've been wracking my brains out trying to figure out that out too. But more than that, I'm dying to know how in the hell Chantal's lawyer is going to maneuver her out this bullshit."

"**Good afternoon, Chantal, have a seat,**" the distinguished looking attorney said. "Can I get you something?"

"No thank you, I'm fine," she lied.

"How are you holding up? I know how tough things have been but we're making progress," he said confidently.

"Really? Tell me more, Mitchell. I need some good news."

"I believe this insanity plea just might work. After my investigators interviewed the officers that arrested you that night, one said that he made the statement that you might end up in the loony bin. They agreed that you seemed awfully delusional."

It aggravated Chantal that people were referring to her as nutty, but if it could get her off then so be it. "But is that enough?"

"It's a great start. The fact that the initial reaction of the arresting officers was that you were crazy would make it seem more believable to a jury. It isn't beneficial for them to lie for you. Plus my team has been dropping well placed leaks to certain news programs, and the media outlets are actually starting to see you as a victim too. Of course the amount of sympathy you receive will never reach the level of Tyler Blake. She is the real victim, but at least you're not being seen as the villain."

"If people don't see me as the villain, then who is?"

"Andre Jackson of course—if this case makes it to trial, which I'm hoping it won't. We can't drag Tyler through the mud. The jury would hate us. But it's open season on Andre Jackson."

"Not make it to trial, how would that happen?" Chantal asked, not seeing how that would be possible.

"I'm hoping we can plead this out."

"Plead out! Mitchell, I don't want to go to jail! I would rather take my chances with a jury."

"My dear, I would never settle for jail time. I'm thinking a short stint in a mental facility, probation, and community service. I'm scheduling you for a psychiatric evaluation with a top specialist. Your case will be so well prepared that hopefully we'll shake some sense into those prosecutors before they waste a ton of taxpayers' hard earned money on a long drawn out trial."

Chantal left Mitchell Stern's office with newfound hope. She heard he was the best, but if he could get her off without a trial or jail time then he was damn near a miracle worker.

Chantal still couldn't figure out who was footing her legal bills. After the longest week of her life sitting in jail, Mr. Stern appeared out the clear blue sky. At first the Judge had denied bail, and like magic Mitchell not only got that changed, but he also came up with the money. When she insisted on knowing who had hired him and put up the money, he simply told her someone who had her best interest at heart. Chantal didn't know anyone who had pockets that deep who gave a shit about her besides Andre, and she would swear on her life it wasn't him. But who—that was truly the million dollar question.

Tyler felt like a new woman after having a masseuse and a pair of women from her favorite spa come over and pamper her. She got the deluxe treatment and she was now so fresh and so clean.

Tyler had Chrissie bring over some sexy lingerie she ordered from her favorite spot, La Perla. She planned on making love to Andre tonight for the first time since the accident. Tyler finally felt beautiful again and wanted to share her happiness with Andre.

When he came home she was lying in their Clive Christian hand painted cream canopy bed with vanilla candles surrounding the room. The moon was cascading a light that had her body luminous. "Baby, I've been waiting for you," Tyler purred, sliding her body out of the bed.

"I wasn't expecting this, but I'm pleasantly surprised. You look unbelievable. You feel unbelievable," he said, gliding his hand down her exfoliated skin. He placed his face under her neck breathing in the lethal aroma of her perfume. "Oh, Tyler I've been dying to be inside you again. I just didn't want to rush you. I wanted to make sure you were ready," Andre whispered in her ear.

"I'm ready. My body is calling for you," she said seductively, leading Andre to the bed. She pulled his taupe colored silk and cashmere blend turtleneck over his head revealing his chiseled dark almond colored arms and torso. Tyler practically tore off his wife beater so her tongue could explore his carved chest and diamond-hard abs.

"Ohh, Tyler!" he moaned as her tongue made circles around his hard nipples. "Baby, stop, let me please you," Andre said, feeling as if he should be the one bringing Tyler this sort of pleasure.

"No. When I please you it pleases me," Tyler said, now unzipping Andre's jeans. When she finally reached his manhood it was rock hard and perfectly smooth. Before she tasted him she let her hands get lost on his firm sculpted buttocks and used that grip to guide him inside her mouth. It was as if Tyler was famished and she couldn't get his penis further down her throat. She wanted to swallow every part of him and Andre could feel her energy. It aroused him to the point he felt out of control. Instead of being gentle with Tyler the way his mind reasoned he should, he wrapped his hand around her frail neck and pushed her back on the bed. But once he dove inside of her, the warmth and serenity of her pussy calmed him. He tenderly rocked inside of her and passionately kissed her soft lips. He followed her lead as she rolled her body so she could ride him like the black stallion he was. Andre watched her willowy torso move in rhythm as her voluptuous breasts bounced to the beat that was buzzing in his head. He couldn't believe this beautiful creature was his. When both reached their climax in unison, they wrapped their bodies around each other tightly until they fell into a deep sleep.

Chantal sat on her living room couch watching some new modeling reality show. She wondered why it always seemed that the black girls they picked for these sorts of shows had the jacked up weaves and the goofiest smiles. She figured it was some sort of conspiracy to make Americans think these women actually represented African American beauty. *Oh please!* Chantal said to herself. She knew beauty and they weren't it. In the middle of her sizing up the finalist her phone started ringing. "Hello."

"What's up, Chantal? I was calling to check on you," Shari said.

"Girl, I'm watching this simple ass modeling reality show. Shari, you need to be on there competing for that million dollar contract and layout in the magazine. You look more like a model than any of these chicks. One of the hosts on here talking about no matter who wins that all the women should know they are the cream of the crop. What crop are they plucking from? These shows kill me," Chantal said, smacking her lips.

"I'm glad you can be so upbeat under the circumstances." As long as Shari and Chantal had been friends, Shari could never quite understand how Chantal's crazy mind worked.

"You mean facing all that jail time? I actually had a meeting with my attorney a few days ago and he is feeling optimistic with our temporary insanity defense."

"Well you have to be insane to try and run over your ex-fiancé."

"I'm serious, Shari."

"What, you think, I'm joking? I'm serious too. When I first heard about it, I just knew it was a bad joke. Never in a billion years did I think you would seriously try to kill Andre."

"Shari, like I told you before I just lost it. Seeing him and Tyler holding and kissing each other on what was supposed to be our wedding day just made me snap. I only planned to go over there and beg Andre to reconsider taking me back, but when I arrived and saw him with that bitch, I realized the reason he didn't want to get married was because he got back his little princess. I couldn't take it anymore. I put my all into Andre and then that snake came along and snatched him up. The nerve of her!"

"Damn, Chantal, who did you mean to run over? By the way you're talking it seems you did hit the intended victim," Shari said, baffled by her best friend's statements.

"Honestly, in a perfect world I would've run over both of them," Chantal stated matter of factly.

When Tyler woke up the next morning she was rejuvenated and alive. Great sex is definitely the cure for a quick recovery. She wished Andre could've made love to her again this morning but she knew he left early for an important meeting, which she also had. William Donovan, Chrissie and her manager were all coming over shortly to discuss what basically summed up to spin control.

Tyler took a quick shower and put on a comfortable pink terry cloth jogging suit. When she went downstairs she was happy to see that the maid prepared the pastries, and fruit platter with bottled waters, and her favorite mimosa. She heard the door bell ringing right on time. No doubt it was William. He was a punctual freak.

"I'll get it!" she yelled so the maid wouldn't bother coming to the door. "Good morning, William," Tyler said with a beaming smile on her face. She was actually ecstatic to see her mentor and former lover.

"Good morning, beautiful. You look incredible."

"I feel incredible."

"Great. Then you won't mind me telling you how crazy you are for being with that Andre Jackson. I don't understand, Tyler, a woman who has the potential to have it all, throwing her life away for a two bit thug."

"I knew you were going to grill me, but damn, can we at least sit down first?" From the look on William's face, Tyler quickly reasoned William wanted to discuss it now. "Listen, William, I'm not throwing my life away. I know you don't want to hear this but I'm in love."

"My darling Tyler," he said lovingly rubbing her face. "It's that naïveté that makes you a star."

"Help yourself to the goodies," Tyler said, ignoring his comment and going to answer the door. Chrissie and her manager arrived together. Although she loved all three of her team members in their own way, the quicker she wrapped up this meeting the quicker she could get them out of her house.

"Wow, Tyler you look fabulous!" her flaming, delightful manager Felipe gushed. "Doesn't she look awesome, Chrissie?"

"Yes she does, but I saw her yesterday, so unlike you, we had our moment."

As Tyler led them in the living room where William had made himself comfortable, Chrissie and Felipe went straight for the alcohol-laced mimosa while health conscious William sipped his bottled water, just as Tyler expected.

William stood up and passed out a perfectly typed letter to everyone. "This is an outline of what I propose we do for the next six months regarding Tyler's career." They all took a few minutes to read over the well detailed plan. As always, William meticulously covered everything. He was truly ten people in one person. "I know it seems like a lot, but now that I've seen you Tyler, I'm more confident than ever you can handle it."

"This movie that you want to start filming next month, is it the one starring T-Roc?"

"Yes. Why, do you have a problem with that?"

"I'm not sure. You know how Andre feels about T-Roc. I don't think he'll be happy about this."

"Tyler, this is business," Chrissie said before William had a chance to speak his mind. "You have to be able to separate the two."

"I understand that, but Andre and I are getting married and he will be my husband. I have to take his feelings into consideration."

"Married! You can't be serious! His fiancée almost killed you. He is surrounded by unstable and shady people. Marrying him would be the biggest mistake of your life. Even Jennifer Lopez had enough sense to get rid of that deadweight P. Diddy before he ruined her career. Please don't jeopardize your future for that lowlife thug," William warned.

"I have to agree, Tyler, especially after this tragedy. You're lucky to be alive," Chrissie added.

"You don't have an opinion, Felipe?" Tyler asked sarcastically.

"Tyler, sweetie, you know I'm a romantic. Plus, I'm wise enough to know that you can't change the heart. I'll support you with whatever decision you make."

17

Both Chrissie and William gave Felipe the look of death. But Tyler knew he didn't care. Felipe had too many neurotic relationships to pass judgment on anybody.

"I appreciate that, Felipe. I also appreciate both of your concerns," Tyler said, looking at Chrissie and William. "But I need you both to respect my decision. Andre is the man I want to be with. I will do the film with T-Roc and your other long list of commitments, William. So can't we compromise?" Tyler asked, giving William the smile she knew he could never resist.

"Whatever you say. The last thing I want to do is upset my star. You have a busy schedule ahead of you. 'Angel' is premiering at the end of the month so you and your significant other have a lot of press ahead of you."

"William, I don't understand why the studio isn't pushing the film back. Especially since I just got home from the hospital and I'm surrounded by all this media because of that psycho, Chantal."

"There you go. The studio is trying to milk the publicity for all it's worth. They couldn't have paid for a better setup. You're on the front page of every magazine and the top headline for every tabloid show. To the studio execs this is the perfect opportunity. If it wasn't for the fact that you're my best friend I would agree with them from a publicity standpoint. But I know how this is affecting you," Chrissie explained.

Tyler stood up and walked towards the window overlooking the beach. She wanted to run in the water and get swept away by the waves. She honestly didn't know how much more she could take.

"Tyler, I know this is hard but you have to be strong. Eventually this too shall pass," William said, reading her mind. If only he could make it pass now.

Chapter Three

Sweet Sacrifice

T-Roc was looking forward to meeting with William Donovan. The untitled movie project he was about to embark on was long overdue. There seemed to be one stumbling block after another. First Andre unjustly stole what should have been his starring role in 'Angel'. Then when William finally gave the green-light for T-Roc to star in his next movie with Tyler, crazy ass Chantal ran the chick over. The last thing T-Roc wanted was some long drawn out trial, and with Chantal sitting in jail and ending up with a lackluster attorney or worse, a court appointed defense lawyer, the case would've dragged on forever. That's why he took it upon himself to hire Mitchell Stern to handle the case. Stern would turn the whole ordeal into a circus that neither Tyler nor Andre would want any part of. T-Roc rationalized that Tyler would become so overwhelmed by the media coverage she would want the whole thing to just go away. And Andre would feel so torn, because although he was in love with Tyler, Chantal was the mother of his child. Sending her to jail and leaving his daughter without a mother would be hard on even the coldest hearted man. If it all worked out the way he imagined, Chantal would do a Paris Hilton and get off with a slap on the wrist. Her freedom would eventually drive a wedge between Andre and Tyler. While working on the movie with Tyler he would be there to console her and soon they would be the King and Queen of Hollywood. Oh if only it could work out that smoothly, T-Roc hoped.

     "Good morning. I'm here for my meeting with William Donovan," T-Roc said to the secretary. He glanced around the office space and liked William's style. There was nothing ghetto fabulous about his taste; it was upscale and classy. I suppose like the man himself.

     "Just one moment sir."

A few moments later William came out and greeted him. "Hi, T-Roc, it's good to see you," William said as they walked to his office. "Have a seat." T-Roc rubbed his hands together as he sat down anticipating good news. "I must say I'm awfully excited about this movie." It was clear to T-Roc that William was telling the truth because of the big smile on his face. "It's an urban version of 'Pretty Woman' with flavor, and instead of the leading lady being a prostitute she's a struggling actress on the rise. You see what the role did for Julia Roberts. I have no doubt in my mind it will do the exact same—if not more—for Tyler. Of course your spin on the Richard Gere character will make you the most sought after leading man in Hollywood since… I guess me in my prime. This is the kind of vehicle that will make everyone shine, if it's done properly."

T-Roc sat attentively listening to William. He always respected the Oscar winner as an actor but he was also digging his business skills. William knew what he was doing. There were no half ass street movies coming from him. Everything was top of the line. He wanted minority actors to shine in a way Hollywood wasn't used to. His movies had glamour and well written storylines. T-Roc knew he could learn a lot from the Tinsel Town icon and felt good to be on his team.

"So what do you think, T-Roc?"

"I think it's fantastic. This is just the type of role I've been waiting for. Although I have to admit I was very disappointed that I didn't get the part as Damian in 'Angel'."

"I know, so was I. But young man, in life there is a reason for everything. It took me many years to accept that fact. Once I did, the world was mine. I know you wanted 'Angel', but now you have this. 'Angel' will no doubt make Tyler a bigger star, but the movie she is doing with you will make her a superstar. If you play your cards right it can do the same for you."

"No doubt. How is Tyler doing anyway? It's so tragic what happened to her. A sweet girl like that shouldn't have to deal with so much drama. I know with this whole trial hanging over her head it has to be stressful," T-Roc said, fishing for information.

"Yeah, it is," William said, tapping the pen on his mahogany desk. "I'm hoping it won't come to a trial. There is good publicity, and then there is too much publicity on a bad situation. Right now the outpour of sympathy is doing wonderful things for Tyler's image, but a long trial might tarnish her golden girl status. Chantal has one of, if not the best, LA criminal attorney. How she maneuvered that is still a mystery, but regardless, he plays hardball. I'm sure he will pull out all the stops to make Chantal appear as the victim; the betrayed and heartbroken fiancée who went ballistic because her long time boyfriend and father of her child had dumped her on their wedding day for beautiful starlet, Tyler Blake. The public might see Tyler as a selfish Hollywood home wrecker. You never know what these jurors are thinking. But honestly, too much time and money has been put into Tyler for us to even take that chance."

"I can understand your concern, William. Also, with a trial I'm sure it will be difficult for Andre to testify against the mother of his child."

"Don't even get me started on that son-of-a-bitch! He is the reason for all of Tyler's problems. What I wouldn't give to have him out of Tyler's life once and for all."

Those closing remarks was all T-Roc needed to hear, to know that his plan might just work out indeed. He was patiently plotting for just the right time to reveal the newly discovered skeleton his informant pulled out of Andre's closet. T-Roc was waiting for the perfect opportunity to play his cards. When he did, T-Roc had no doubt it would be *adios* for Andre Jackson.

Tyler was lying on the couch reading through the movie script William had delivered yesterday. She was impressed and actually excited to get back to work. Of course Andre thought it was too soon and he really exploded when she revealed T-Roc was her leading man. After a long heart to heart he finally understood that it was business.

They also finally spoke about their baby that Tyler lost. Andre was actually taking it harder than her. He felt solely responsible for the loss of their child. In his mind if he'd never agreed to marry Chantal in the first place, he wouldn't have triggered any of the tragedies that followed.

Tyler tried her best to reassure him that he wasn't the blame. They decided after filming her movie with T-Roc they would work on starting a family. That was something Tyler was looking forward to.

"You scared me! I didn't even hear you come in," she said after the touch of Andre's lips on her forehead pulled her out of daydreaming.

"What had your mind so far away?" Andre wanted to know.

"Actually I was thinking about the beautiful babies we're going to make together."

"Yeah, I've been thinking about that too. But I was thinking about all the fun we would have making the beautiful babies," he said grinning. Andre walked over to the bar and poured himself a drink.

"Andre, you're having a double shot of Cognac in the middle of the day. What has you so stressed?"

Even before Tyler finished her question Andre was pouring his second glass. "I didn't want to tell you this but they'll be calling you anyway."

"Who are they?"

"The District Attorney's office. I had to meet with them today," he revealed with frustration in his voice.

"Why didn't you tell me?"

"I didn't want you to worry. The last thing you need to agonize about is this fucking case. This bullshit is driving me crazy."

"Andre, what's wrong?" Tyler asked, concerned with the torture on his face.

Andre just stood quiet for a minute with his head down, rubbing his chin. "Chantal's snake ass lawyer is really trying to do a number on me. The DA told me how he's basically going to put me on trial. Talking about I'm a drug addict and I got Chantal hooked on drugs. That I physically and mentally abused her which drove her insane and caused her to have a nervous breakdown and try to kill me."

"What?" Tyler said, just feeling the walls closing in on her.

"Tyler, I ain't no saint, never claimed to be. But I've never laid a hand on Chantal. Yeah, we dabbled in drugs and would get fucked up, but neither of us was addicted. I know I wasn't. Chantal was a party girl before I met her. Yeah, I did fuck around on her a lot, but she knew what type of dude I was before she locked me down with our daughter. I was never in love with Chantal and she knew it. They are going to try to paint me out to be some monster. The DA said he would try to make it so a lot of that stuff is inadmissible, but they'll find a way to get it in. My family, my daughter is going to hear that attorney try to tear me down, and then I'm going to have to turn around and tear Chantal down. That woman disgusts me, but to be honest with you, Tyler, there is so much pain in my heart because I do feel responsible."

Tyler could see the hurt in his eyes, and it was killing her. "Andre, I don't know what to say. I'll admit that I've had nightmares about going to court and facing the million questions they will throw at me, but it doesn't compare to the havoc they'll throw at you. I feel terrible that you're in such a no win situation."

"Don't feel sorry for me. You're the one that was in the hospital damn near on your death bed for over a month and lost our baby because of my immature behavior."

"What do you mean your immature behavior?"

"Don't you understand that I did mislead Chantal and treated her like shit? I used her because I couldn't have the woman I really wanted, which was you. When she slit her wrist that was a clear sign she was off her rocker. Then I turn around because you say you don't want us to be together and I ask her to marry me, knowing I didn't give a fuck about her in that way. I'm a bastard, because as soon as you came back I tossed her to the side like she was nothing. The crazy part is, if you hadn't come back I would've married the conniving broad. She would've been overjoyed finally being Mrs. Andre Jackson and I'd still been pinning over you and fucking mad other bitches to avoid facing my miserable existence."

Tyler was shocked by the rawness of what Andre was saying. He was judging himself in a light that she could've never seen him in, but at the same time it did make a lot of sense. They fell in love so fast that she didn't have the opportunity to know or understand that part of Andre. The self destructive man that was trying to take responsibility for his less than stellar past behavior, it made her love him even more. The truth be told, Tyler didn't know if she could be so honest about her own checkered past or the emotional baggage she still carried around.

"Why are you looking at me like that?" Andre finally asked after Tyler sat staring at him.

"I was somewhere else for a minute," Tyler said, now standing up pouring herself something to drink. "Andre, I admire the fact that you're being so candid about your feelings. What do you want to do? I mean honestly. I'm so tired of turning on the television and seeing our names splashed across the headlines over this bullshit. It's a nightmare. Maybe something can be worked out where a trial can be avoided. I definitely don't want to become infamous as the actress who was hit by the deranged would be bride," Tyler said, finding laughter in the whole incident for the first time.

"You're too much. What are you saying that you want to end this?"

"I've *been* wanting to end this," Tyler remarked, stressing the word been. "I don't think that Chantal should walk away free as a bird, but if we can avoid a trial, then by all means let's make it happen."

For a moment Andre felt like this was the beginning of putting the whole Chantal nightmare behind them, but he wasn't sure if Tyler was saying this because that's how she felt or if she wanted to protect him. He didn't want to pressure Tyler into doing something she didn't want to do, especially since out of the three of them she truly didn't deserve any of this. "Tyler, I want you to really think this over carefully before you make any decisions. I'll admit, I don't want to get caught up in some freak show trial, but if you want Chantal to pay for her actions then I will see this through with you until the very end."

Tyler walked towards Andre and kissed him lightly on the lips. Then she gazed in his eyes and could see how sincere his words were. She knew that he would stand by her side even if it meant unlimited scrutiny and breaking the heart of his family, especially his daughter. Tyler couldn't allow that to happen. The love she felt for Andre ran way too deep. "Baby, listen. A major part of me wants Chantal to rot in jail. She has to be the most destructive woman I've ever encountered. But at the same time, part of me can understand her pain. In Chantal's mind you all truly belong together and I came along and ruined everything. She has to be dying inside thinking about all of the what ifs, and I know that has to hurt you too."

"But I don't want you doing this for me. You were the one that got hit by a car and almost died. I have no right to ask you to protect me."

"I'm not protecting you, I'm doing what I believe is best for us. Even though we're not married yet, we're family, and one day Melanie will be my step daughter. Just like you don't want her to resent you, I don't want her to resent me either. Chantal does need to get help, but Melanie deserves to have her mother in her life."

"You continue to amaze me. What did I do to ever be blessed with a woman like you? You really are too good for me."

"My sentiments exactly," Tyler said before being distracted by the sound of clicking heels. Both she and Andre turned their heads to see who the unexpected guest was.

"Mother! What are you doing here?"

"That's a silly question. I'm not supposed to come see my daughter?"

"How long have you've been standing there?" Tyler asked, feeling annoyed that her mother was interrupting a serious conversation between her and Andre.

"Long enough to know you're planning on letting that nut job that tried to run you over get off with a slap on the wrist. I can't decide who needs to be institutionalized, you or that Chantal Morgan."

"Woman, enough already," Andre barked, unable to contain the built up anger he had towards her.

"Don't you speak to me in that tone, you minuscule thug!"

Before the firecrackers could start, Tyler intervened. "Mother, stop!"

"You need to tell him to stop. He's the one to blame for all this nonsense."

"No he's not."

"Tyler, you don't have to defend me to your mother or anybody else," Andre said as he held Tyler's hand. He then turned to Maria. "I apologize for how I spoke to you, but only because you're the mother of the woman I'm in love with and who I plan to make my wife. I don't take kindly to anybody speaking to me in a derogatory manner, and that includes you. I understand that you're concerned about your daughter's welfare, but so am I. So when you come into our home, you treat me with respect or visit your daughter off of these premises. Now that I've made that clear, I'll give you two ladies some time alone." Andre gave Tyler a kiss on the lips before making his way upstairs.

"The nerve of him to make such a threat to me!" Maria said once Andre was no longer within earshot.

"He didn't threaten you, Mother, he simply stated the facts. Whether you like it or not, Andre and I are together. We will be husband and wife and you need to accept that. And I won't tolerate you disrespecting him, especially not in his own home."

"How can you pick him over your mother?"

"This isn't a contest. I'm not picking Andre over you. This is more about respect than anything else. Just like I would never allow him to degrade you, I'm just asking you to please respect the man I love. Is that really asking too much?"

Tyler is asking entirely too much of me. But I've lived long enough and know Tyler well enough not to push any further. The last thing I want to do is alienate her and I can feel that I'm beginning to do just that. If I want to get rid of Andre, I have to make Tyler value my advice and that means first gaining her trust, Maria thought to herself.

"My sweet, beautiful daughter, I'm so sorry I've upset you. I just adore you so. If Andre is the man you want to spend the rest of your life with then I will respect your wishes."

"You mean that?"

"Of course I do. You know I never say anything that I don't mean. I promise to be polite to my future son-in-law, and to actually try to make amends."

"Mother, you're the best. Thank you so much. For my mother and future husband to be close, that would mean the world to me."

"I know it would. So don't you worry, my little princess. Mother will make it right," Maria said as she hugged her daughter.

Little did Tyler know that making it right meant Andre had to go, if it was the last thing Maria Chambers had to do.

Chapter Four

Infatuation

It was a Friday night and Chantal was feeling more than alright. Earlier that day she met with her attorney, Mitchell Stern and he had given her some very promising news. After weeks of going back and forth, he was finally making some constructive leeway with the District Attorney who was prosecuting her case. Initially after he offered to have the charges reduced, he insisted that Chantal do some jail time. But Chantal had been decided that was out of the question, and her attorney agreed with her one hundred percent.

To show he meant business, Mitchell had Chantal do an exclusive interview with Larry King. Of course all the questions were given to Chantal in advance and she was well rehearsed on what to say. And with her attorney right by her side the interview went off more smoothly than even Mitchell had anticipated. The thousands of dollars spent on a media trainer had more than paid off. Chantal came off as poised, intelligent and a victim of love. Not only did she have Larry King eating out the palm of her hands, so were the callers:

"Ms. Morgan, I sympathize with you for what happened on what was supposed to be your wedding day, but can you explain how it drove you to try and run over your ex fiancé?" a caller asked.

Chantal let out a passive sigh and stared at Larry King for an endearing moment, and then turned to the camera as if speaking directly to the caller. "Have you ever been so in love with a man that you lose your sense of better judgment? Well, that's what happened with Andre. He is the father of my child and I believed we would spend the rest of our lives together. I feel horrible for the mistake I made, but I was a victim of love…"

The next morning the District Attorney was almost begging to get the case closed. Not only was his office getting hundreds of calls in support of Chantal, but Tyler's and Andre's mouth pieces wanted damage control on all the bad press the two were getting, especially since their Hollywood premiere of 'Angel' was right around the corner.

Chantal was snapping her fingers to the music as she and Shari drove down Sunset Blvd. headed to the club. "Money can truly buy freedom, I can attest to that," Chantal belted over the loud music."

Shari turned down the volume unable to hear what Chantal said. "Repeat that. I couldn't hear you."

"I said, money can truly buy freedom," Chantal beamed.

"I'm assuming you're talking about yourself, and you damn right. I still can't get over the turn of events. God forbid, but if I ever get caught up in some mess, please let me have Mr. Stern to the rescue. His bill gotta be ridiculous."

"I wouldn't know. I still haven't seen one."

"You still don't know who's been kicking out all that bread to your attorney?"

"Hell no, and at this particular point I don't even care. Just as long as the bills keep getting paid, what the fuck ever."

"But you got to be curious about who is spending this type of dough to keep you out of the slammer. You sure it ain't Andre?"

Chantal gave Shari the gangsta look. "Bitch, now you know that asshole ain't helping me with shit. He so wrapped up in that Tyler Blake he probably forgot what I look like."

"I doubt that. After Larry King, a few motherfuckers know what you look like, and I know Andre saw you on there just like everybody else."

"Yeah, well regardless, he wouldn't dare be footing my bill. I don't know who my secret Santa is, but whoever it is the angels were truly looking out for me on this one."

"So what's next with the case?"

"Thelma, that is why we're going out to party tonight because I'm this close to getting off with probation. Plus, the two lovebirds have their movie premiere tonight and I don't want to be sitting at home thinking about that."

"Girl, you fucked me up with that one. You haven't called me Thelma in like forever. I know that's right."

"Okay, we are always going to be Thelma and Louise out this bitch. Them chicks were official just like us." Chantal and Shari did their little pinky shake and burst out laughing.

"So wait, back to what you were saying. They are trying to give you probation without you going away to the mental hospital or nothing?" Shari asked in shock.

"Yes, honey. Like some outpatient program. I would still have to meet with a doctor for therapy sessions, but I would see him like three times a week and then take my ass home. As the doctor felt I was getting better my sessions would become less and less. And you know with all my charm, he'll be writing my discharge papers before you can say 'Psycho'.

"But what if it isn't a man, then what?"

"Oh, Mitchell has that covered. In the plea deal he's working it out that I'm in a private facility, and since I will pay the cost he will find three suitable doctors for the prosecutors to chose from. All of them will be heterosexual males, trust."

"Chantal, you're too much. It's not safe for you to be out on the streets, but I mean that in the most endearing way."

Chantal couldn't help but laugh at Shari's statement because she meant it as a joke, but it surly had an underlining truth to it.

"Baby, how do I look?" Tyler asked, twirling around in her couture white sapphire Monique Lhuillier gown.

"Incredible! You really do look like an angel."

"You always know exactly what to say to make me feel good," Tyler said, rubbing the tip of her nose on the tip of Andre's nose. "As always we're running late, so we better go."

"Wait, you're forgetting something."

"What?" Tyler questioned as she looked herself up and down. "I have my purse and I can't fit anything else in this dress."

"What about something around your neck?" Andre said as he pulled out a Harry Winston box.

When Tyler opened the box her eyes popped when she saw the diamond oval drop necklace. "Omigoodness, it's gorgeous! I had no idea Harry Winston was loaning me a diamond necklace for the premiere. Wow, this is amazing! Baby, put it on for me." Tyler admired herself in the mirror as the necklace complimented her dress perfectly. "This is the most beautiful necklace I've ever seen. I wish I could keep it forever."

"You can."

"No, seriously, you know how much a necklace like this cost?"

"Yeah, especially since I paid for it."

"What!" Tyler screamed, surprised by what Andre said.

"It's my gift to you. Diamonds are forever and so are we."

"Don't do this."

"Do what?"

"Don't make me cry right before it's time to go. The makeup artist is gone and there is no way I can touch up my face."

"Don't cry. We can't have that. I want you looking like the movie star you are when you walk down that red carpet. Save those tears for tonight when I'm inside you and you're crying out my name from the pleasure I'm giving you."

"I love you so much. There'll never be another man for me."

"Better not be." Andre slid his fingers through Tyler's hand and they left to see the movie where they fell in love.

"**Girl, this spot, Les Deux is** hot! I'm feeling this LA scene. It's not on fire like New York but it's cool. It has another kind of flavor," Shari said as she glanced around the spot.

"Yeah, I like LA too. So much that I'm considering moving out this way."

"What, and leave Chicago?"

"I would keep my house but also get a place here where I would spend the majority of my time. I know Melanie would love it here too, and she could also be near Andre more. I'm sure now that he's going to be a movie star and is marrying one, he'll be spending most of his time in LA."

"Chantal, I love you to death, you're like a sister to me, but you have to stop building your life around Andre. Because LA is his home, you want it to be your home too. It's time to move on and put Andre behind you."

"I'm not following Andre around. We do have a child together."

"Yeah, and a lot of kids grow up with their parents in two different states, that's why they have stuff like visitation rights. If I remember correctly, while you were living in Chicago Andre was living in New York. So no, you don't have to move here so he can be closer to his daughter. It sounds as if once again you're using Melanie to stalk her father. You need to just stop. I'm telling you this because I love you, Chantal, not to hurt you."

There was no need for Shari to even justify what she was saying. Chantal knew for a fact that Shari was her best friend. All the shit that they had been through together, there was nothing but unconditional love between them. "I hear everything you're saying, Shari. And believe it or not, I'm listening too."

"That's all I ask. Now pour me some more of that bubbly and let's make a toast."

"Wait, hold up a minute," Chantal said, zooming in on some guys that just sat down at a booth across the floor from them. "Is that Ian Addison that just walked up in here?"

"Where? That motherfucker fine as shit. He in here?" Shari questioned, wanting to get a good look at the heavily hyped athlete.

"I think so, right across over there," Chantal said, nudging Shari's arm but still trying to be discreet.

It didn't matter though, because nobody was paying attention to them. All eyes were on Ian Addison and his crew. After Shaq was traded to Miami, they brought Ian to the Lakers to be Kobe's partner. They have been dominating the West Coast ever since. The fans and media couldn't get enough of the good looking pair and the women especially loved the charismatic Ian Addison. When he smiled it seemed as if the whole basketball court lit up.

"Girl, that is him and he is even finer in person than on television! I would do anything to wake up next to that every morning. Oh shit, that's Jalen Griffin with him too!"

"That name sounds familiar."

Yeah, he was the first round draft pick last year and signed that ridiculous eighty million dollar Nike contract. Girl, I would welcome either one of those cats in my bed."

"That ain't nothing but the truth. You know that Ian used to be Tyler's man," Chantal informed Shari.

"Tyler Blake?"

"Yes, what other Tyler do we know?" Chantal mocked sarcastically.

"Damn, she has fucked with some prime dick. But how did she let Ian Addison go?" Shari licked her lips as if she was about to serve him up on a plate.

"I don't know all that. But what I do know was there was a time she was going hot and heavy with him. You remember Keshia?"

"Yeah, one of our semi homegirls from around the way."

"Hum hun, well she used to fuck with some guy that played on the team with Ian when he first got in the league. When they had games in Chicago I would go with her to see him play and Tyler would be there. So I asked Keisha about her because after the games they would be all up on each other like they were tighter than those jeans you got on."

"So what did Keisha tell you?" Shari asked, becoming impatient with Chantal's long winded inside scoop.

"Well, she said that even when that dude she was fucking with would fly her out sometimes, Tyler would still be right there. The dude on his team told her that Tyler was Ian's woman and he even heard rumors one time that they were going to get married. Why cats want to marry that silly broad is beyond me."

"Yo, that shit is crazy. But I heard he did get married a couple of years ago."

"Me too, but from what my sources tell me he's already headed to divorce court. He had a baby with the chick and decided to take a walk down the aisle, but from what I understand he realized he picked the wrong aisle, or better yet, the wrong girl to stroll down it with."

"She be alright when they get that divorce. I'm sure she'll be getting a nice piece of change," Shari reasoned.

"Think again. From what they tell me, before he even put the engagement ring on her finger his lawyers had an airtight pre-nup drawn up. I don't know what exactly is in it but she not walking away with much. She was just so happy to be marrying his fine ass she didn't care what it said."

"But can you blame her; he is one slice of perfection."

Both women sat there scheming on how they could make their move, along with every other female in the club.

Tyler was overwhelmed when she stepped out of the Limo and the paparazzi swarmed her. She was so relieved that Andre was right by her side. But what amazed her even more were the thousands of fans lined up against the ropes screaming her name and begging for an autograph. Tyler was used to fans but not this many. They were chanting her name as if she had been staring in movies all her life. Chrissie immediately came up to Tyler and Andre to walk them down the red carpet and for them to speak to the press that was waiting to get a quick interview.

"Wait, I want to speak to my fans and sign a few autographs before going in," Tyler insisted.

"Tyler, you really don't have time."

"Well, make time." Before Chrissie could say another word Tyler grabbed Andre's hand and began waving and shaking hands with her adoring fans. Andre got caught up in the moment and began doing the same. They signed autographs and the crowd went wild. The security was surrounding the couple trying to keep the hordes of people under control.

"That's enough, baby. We really have to go now."

"Okay," Tyler said with slight resistance. This was the life she always dreamed of. Her name up in bright lights at her movie premiere and adoring fans chanting her name. She never wanted the moment to end.

From a distance T-Roc watched as the new 'It' couple of Hollywood signed autographs and smiled for the cameras. It burned him up that Andre was the one shining in all his glory. That was supposed to be him holding Tyler's hand and speaking to the press. But soon he knew his day would come. Next week T-Roc and Tyler would start filming their own movie and he would seize the opportunity to win back the woman he was determined to make his own once and for all. "Yeah Andre, enjoy this moment because it won't last. Once I unleash the sordid secrets of your past you'll be like the plague in this city," T-Roc grinned, relishing in Andre's impending demise.

"Let's go dance," Chantal said, grabbing Shari's arm and heading to the dance floor when T.I.'s new club banger started roaring out of the sound system. Chantal began doing her best Beyonce booty dance to the crazy hot beat as all the fellas were eyeing her, even the ones who were with their girlfriends. That was all cool to Chantal, but she was only interested in catching the eye of one fella in particular.

Shari coolly danced to the music, keeping a close eye on Chantal. She knew exactly what she was up to from the moment she wanted to hit the dance floor. See, Chantal never liked being all in the crowd dancing with everybody else. She thought she was too elite for that. She preferred to be dancing at a spot around her booth, or if she was really feeling herself, on the table. But she wanted to go to the dance floor to be as close to Ian as possible without it looking too obvious. Chantal hoped that once he saw her dropping it like it's hot that he would become enamored and invite her to have a drink at his table.

Shari had seen Chantal play this same game several times before, but for whatever reason it didn't seem to be working. If Ian was checking for Chantal then he was keeping it under wraps. That didn't deter Chantal though; she started twisting her torso even harder to the music and sticking out her shapely ass with more grind. And finally it seemed that her hard work paid off.

"Pretty girl, you sexy as shit. Why don't you and your friend come over and have a drink with us," the tall basketball player asked. He was one of Ian's teammates and sitting at the table with him.

"Maybe Ian didn't ask, but at least I'm one step closer to getting to him," Chantal whispered in Shari's ear as they followed the guy back to his table. Besides him there were four other guys sitting at the table, including Ian.

"Ladies have a seat. I'm Glen and this is Jalen, Kirk, Roger and Ian." The guys all nodded their heads saying what's up.

"I'm Chantal and this is Shari."

"I thought your name was Beyonce the way you was putting it down on that dance floor."

"That's funny," Chantal said, trying to catch a glimpse of Ian. A couple of the other dudes were cute but Chantal had her eye on the number one stunner.

"But seriously, are you some type of entertainer? Because you look mad familiar," one of the other players said, trying to place Chantal's face. The last thing Chantal wanted was for one of them to realize she was the deranged would be bride that tried to mow down her fiancé. Ian could find out all that after she had put it on him in bed.

"No I'm not a famous entertainer yet, but give me some time."

"With moves like you got, there is no doubt that you will be."

They all started laughing and clicking their glasses, except for the one person she wanted to. Chantal was now becoming annoyed. Ian wasn't paying her any attention. He was too busy small talking to some obvious groupie that was all up in his face. The players were now laughing and joking with Shari and getting there champagne campaign on, so Chantal used the opportunity to have a few words with her target.

"Is that what I need to do? Come up and speak in a baby voice and dangle my tits up in your face?" Chantal asked with a seductive twinkle in her eyes.

"Excuse me?" Ian asked, not sure if he heard correctly what the woman sitting next to him said.

"If I want to get your attention do I need to babble in baby talk and dangle my tits up in your face? That's what I said."

"Are you referring to me?" the bimbo looking woman asked, sounding like a complete airhead.

"Yeah, I am. Do you have a problem with that?"

The woman was taken completely aback by Chantal's candidness. She was no fighter and it was obvious she wasn't into drama, because without saying another word she turned around and almost ran away.

"Back to you," Chantal continued as if the woman had never been there.

Ian just sat for a second staring at Chantal. He'd never seen a woman be so raw and cool at the same time. "What about me?"

"You didn't answer my question."

"Oh, about getting my attention, well you definitely have it now."

"How do I keep it?"

Ian let out a slight laugh. "Well that's on you."

"All I need is a chance. Will you give me that?"

"Damn, your approach is a little crazy. I'm used to women coming at me and your style of confidence is different, but I'm feeling it."

"That's all that matters then. I like what I see and I'm hoping you'll give me the opportunity to let you like me too."

"I believe in equal opportunity. But didn't my man invite you to the table?"

"Of course, but I put that show on hoping that you would be the one inviting me to this table."

"So that little performance was for my benefit?"

"And you know that. I'm relieved to know that you noticed me while I was doing my best video vixen dance impression."

"That's cute." Ian was truly digging the honesty that Chantal was spitting. Most women schemed to meet him, but none of them would admit it, so hearing Chantal's confessions was a breath of fresh air. And besides that, Ian had to admit that the woman sitting beside him wanting his attention was drop dead gorgeous. He had noticed her before she even hit the dance floor and was positively impressed with the way she moved her body to the music. The only reason he didn't invite her to have a seat was because besides having a wife, he had two mistresses, a hand full of jump offs and wasn't interested in adding any new blood. Plus he could tell by just looking at Chantal that she was not new to the game. Her appearance was straight perfection. There would be no hit and run with her. She would have to be an official member of his cipher.

"So have you made up your mind?" Chantal asked as if she knew he was debating if he wanted to take it there with her or not.

"Made up my mind about what?"

"Whether or not you want me to make you fall in love."

"You're too much," Ian chuckled.

"Is that a yes or a no?"

"Like I said, I believe in equal opportunity."

"Great. I'll take that as a yes."

"I mean, I'll think about it and get back to you," Ian said as he licked his lips and gave Chantal a hypnotizing stare that almost made her come in her silk panties. But once she snapped out of her trance and digested what she considered a cold diss Ian just gave her, she was mortified. Nobody ever had to contemplate getting an opportunity to feel between Chantal's legs and she was offended that it was starting now.

"Come on Shari, let's go," Chantal said calmly.

Shari was in the middle of drinking her glass of champagne and listening to another one of Jalen's silly jokes. His jokes weren't that funny but all Shari kept focusing on was his basketball sized diamond stud and the pretty dimples that decorated his face every time he smiled. "You ready to go already? But we just sat down!"

Chantal stood. Burning up inside that Ian had just given her the brush off and her best friend was putting her on the spot. She didn't want to light into Shari in front of these guys because she would be playing herself and Ian would know just how bad he got under her skin. Instead, Chantal decided to come up with what she thought was a lady like excuse. "No, I would love to stay longer because I'm having a great time but my stomach is getting nauseated from drinking this champagne. I made the stupid mistake of not eating anything before coming out." Chantal gave a demure smile and the guys nodded their heads as if understanding her dilemma.

But Shari knew better, especially since they had a very expensive Italian cuisine at a restaurant right before coming to the club. She knew that was Chantal's way of saying 'Let's get the fuck out of here now!'"

"Oh, girl, I understand. Let me get my purse so we can go."

"Wait a minute, can I get your number before you leave?" Jalen asked as he put his hand over Shari's hand.

"No doubt." Shari gladly wrote down her digits hoping she would be seeing the sexy basketball player sooner than later. Glen, the guy that originally invited them over was about to ask Chantal for her number, but he had picked up the vibe that she only had interest in Ian.

The two ladies made their way out the booth and Shari could feel the fire coming out of Chantal's head. "Girl, you alright?"

"Hell no! That stupid fuck Ian really tried to play me. No, he did play me."

"What happened?" Shari was beyond curious. She had never seen Chantal this visibly upset over a random prospect. She could only recall Andre having Chantal vexed like this.

"I basically threw myself at that cocky motherfucker and then he had the nerve to tell me he would think about whether he wants to get with me or not. Can you believe that clown?"

"You know he got mad bitches coming at him all the time so it shouldn't be surprising that he feeling himself. You can't really expect any less."

Chantal gave Shari the frown face as if Shari forgot who she was talking to. Chantal didn't even have to say anything, because Shari already knew. Chantal didn't believe those type of rules applied to her. She always put herself on a shelf way above every other woman, which was understandable because with Chantal's bronzed complexion, honey-blonde hair that highlighted her perfectly featured face, and to top it off, a body that wouldn't stop even after having a baby, there was no mistaking she was in an elite class.

"Chantal, don't even stress it. Fuck Mr. NBA. It's his loss," Shari said as the two women waited for the parking valet to pull around their car. The last thing Shari wanted was for Chantal to be in a funk, especially with all she had been going through. Knowing Andre was canoodling with Tyler Blake was already driving her crazy. She surly didn't need the first man she stepped to send her on her way.

Both women stood deliberating on what transpired within the last hour. Shari had a huge grin on her face imagining being wined and dined by Jalen and then having dessert with the good looking 6'4 stud twisting her out.

Chantal was secretly wondering had she lost her edge, and at the ripe age of twenty-six was her beauty fading. She imagined waking up in the middle of the night and walking to the bathroom. When she turned on the light and looked in the mirror her face was full of wrinkles and her once smooth as a babies bottom skin looked like bad leather that had been in the sun too long. Not only that, but she had ballooned to a size twenty-four. Right before she was about to have a panic attack, a pair of strong arms wrapped themselves around the middle of her bare stomach, then took his finger and began playing with her diamond stud belly button ring.

"I thought about it and I would like to give you a try," Ian whispered in her ear giving Chantal chills down her spine. "So you coming with me tonight or what?"

"All you had to do was ask." When the valet pulled up with her car she gave Shari 'the look' topped with a wink and headed off hand-in-hand with Ian.

Chapter Five

Toxic

"Damn, baby, you working that pussy out!" Ian moaned as Chantal rode him seductively. It had been so long since she had a man inside her that Chantal put her mind, body and soul into her lovemaking session with Ian. She savored every stroke as she arched her back and flexed her inner muscles.

Ian had his hands under her buttocks, squeezing them as if they felt like Charmin. He couldn't get over how moist her insides were and he closed his eyes relishing the unbelievable feeling she was giving him. When he opened them and saw Chantal had her eyes closed and was rubbing her breasts as if making love to herself, he became even more aroused.

"Baby, do I feel good inside you?" Ian asked, wanting to hear more than the alluring sigh Chantal was making. He wanted confirmation that he felt just as good to her as she did to him.

"Oh, yes, Ian! I can't get enough of you. You're about to make me come," Chantal uttered as she felt that tingling feeling in her body building up that she had been yearning to experience again for so long.

Ian began stroking her harder in the exact spot he needed to tap. "Baby, yes, right there, right there, you feel so good! Oh, yes I'm about to come baby! Oh *yes!*" Chantal cried out one last time before collapsing on Ian's sweat glistened chest. Chantal's once straightened hair was now drenched from the workout she just put in.

Ian slowly lifted Chantal up and laid her on the side of him. Since it was evident she was exhausted he gazed at Chantal's naked body and then took off his condom before jacking off while rubbing his hands through her hair. By the time he came, Chantal was now ready for part two.

"Didn't we have an amazing night tonight?" Tyler gushed as the Limo driver headed back to their home in Malibu.

"Yeah, I have to admit I truly enjoyed myself. I was a little skeptical about how I would feel seeing myself on a big ass screen with everybody critiquing me, but it wasn't that bad," Andre said as he nodded his head with a proud look on his face.

"See, I knew you would love it. You were awesome. Your scenes with me seemed so sincere."

"They were sincere. The course of our relationship seemed to follow the same path as our characters. When Damian was falling in love with Angel, I was falling in love with you. When Angel started breaking Damian's heart, you were breaking mine."

"Oh, Andre, I'm so sorry. Baby, you know how much I love you and I still loved you even when I was pushing you away. Please forgive me."

Andre put his finger to Tyler's lips. "You don't even have to apologize. We both made mistakes. The important thing is that we found our way back to each other. Everything else is irrelevant."

"I love you so much," Tyler said as she leaned over and passionately kissed Andre. He rolled up the glass window for privacy and the two made love for the duration of their ride home.

T-Roc was looking forward to meeting with Mitchell Stern and delivering what he hoped was his last payment for Chantal's defense. He knew the case would be costly, but never did he expect for the bill to reach the level it was currently at. But Stern was the best criminal attorney in the LA, if not the West Coast. T-Roc felt it was money well spent if all worked out as he planned.

He arrived at the office bright and early so even Stern's secretary wasn't there. He preferred no one seeing him meeting with Stern, and to guarantee that they decided to meet at the crack of dawn.

"T-Roc, always a pleasure," Stern said as he shook T-Roc's hand.

"I'm sure, especially given the amount of money you've made from me," T-Roc said in a playful tone with a touch of sarcasm.

"I think I've earned every dollar," Stern replied with the sly wink he was famous for.

"I'll tell you that after I hear what you have to say." T-Roc sat down anxiously awaiting to hear Stern's report.

"It's a done deal. I reached a final plea agreement with the prosecutor late yesterday afternoon. Chantal won't have to do any jail time, just a long probation, some community service, therapy and pay a rather large fine."

"Have you told Chantal yet?"

"No, I haven't spoken to her, but I figured you should be the first to know, given that your money has bought her freedom. I still don't quite understand why you did all this. You're not romantically involved with Chantal, and from what I understand you're not even friends, so please explain. My curiosity is starting to get the best of me."

"I'm not paying you to have your curiosity quenched, I'm paying you to keep Chantal out of jail, which you've managed to do. I'm very impressed and happy to write you out what I believe is the final check." Stern nodded his head yes as T-Roc gladly pulled out his checkbook to clear up the remaining balance. "This should do it." Stern took a look at all the zeroes and couldn't have agreed more.

"Pleasure doing business with you, T-Roc. Until we meet again." The two shook hands and T-Roc walked out of Stern's office a very happy man.

Chantal woke up feeling like a new woman. Having three orgasms in one night was exactly what she needed to release all of her built up stress. Her sex drive was in high gear and was looking forward to a morning workout, but to her disappointment Ian was still fast asleep. That soon vanished when she got the call from Stern that a plea deal had been worked out and she wouldn't be seeing the inside of a jail cell. Now she no longer wanted to make love to Ian just for pleasure, but also for celebratory reasons.

"Ian, wake up," Chantal said, gently shaking Ian's arm. He had the pillow covering his face and he wasn't budging. She started shaking a little harder until he finally responded.

"What time is it?" he groaned, still not fully awake.

"Eleven o'clock, and time for us to pick up where we left off last night." Chantal rolled over and sat on top of Ian's back hoping that the feel of her warm pussy on his skin would get him aroused.

"Oh shit, I'm late for practice!" Ian jumped up damn near knocking Chantal off the bed. "I can't believe this shit! My fucking alarm didn't even go off."

"Actually it did, but I turned it off," Chantal said innocently.

"So why in the hell didn't you wake me up?'

"You looked so peaceful and I didn't want to disturb you."

"Bitches!" Ian muttered under his breath.

"What the fuck did you just call me?"

"Nothing, forget about it."

"Nah, nigga, I ain't forgetting shit. You ain't been dealing with me long enough to come out your mouth and call me no bitch. You need to check yourself right now."

"That little feisty attitude you got reminds me of this chick I used to deal with. I was trying to figure out what I dug about you so much, and now I know."

"Don't be comparing me to no other bitch you used to fuck with."

"First of all, she's no bitch, and second, take it as a compliment that you even remind me of her."

Chantal couldn't help but catch a case of the green eye monster. She wanted to know who this woman was that he had the nerve to still be thinking about. One thing in her mind she was sure of that it wasn't Tyler Blake. Chantal always figured that Tyler had no backbone, and if anything, she was the timid demure type.

"Whatever, Ian. Just don't call me no bitch anymore."

"I apologize. I just hate being late for practice. I have to take a shower and be out of here."

"Can I join you?"

"As much as I would like that, you'd be a distraction, something I don't have time for."

"So what am I supposed to do? You're obviously in a rush, and I didn't drive over here."

"You got two options. I can either call you a car service or you can wait until I get back. It's up to you. You can decide while I'm in the shower."

Chantal had already decided before he gave her the two options that she wasn't going anywhere. Ian Addison was beyond hot and she planned on making him her man.

Tyler was up going over her script preparing for her first day of shooting tomorrow. Time seemed to be flying and she couldn't believe that she was about to begin filming and T-Roc was her leading man. Tyler already tested with him when he auditioned for the role in Angel, so she knew that he was a good actor and they had undeniable chemistry, which wasn't surprising since they shared a sordid past—a past that she wanted to forget and was happy Andre knew nothing about. Andre already detested T-Roc and didn't want her doing the film with him. If he knew they used to be lovers he would be livid.

"Good morning, baby." Tyler was so caught up thinking about T-Roc that she didn't even hear Andre enter the living room.

"Hi."

"What you reading?"

"That script for my new movie. You know I have to be on set tomorrow."

"Damn, time flies. You start shooting that movie with T-Roc already?"

"Yeah, I was just thinking the same thing. I wish I had another month to relax. It seems like yesterday I got out of the hospital."

"I agree. That's why I think you should postpone starting the movie. You need to give yourself some more time to heal."

"Look at me, Andre. I'm fine." Tyler stood up and did a playful twirl.

"I'm not talking about physically, I'm talking mentally. You went through an unthinkable ordeal. Getting over something like that takes time. You need to think about that."

"That's the thing. I don't want to think about it. Sitting around doing nothing gives me nothing but time to replay the incident over and over again in my head. I want to forget it ever happened and move on with my life. Starting this movie will be a good thing. I can start living my life again. That won't happen until I'm back working and that prosecutor can get a deal worked out with Chantal's attorney. The longer it's lingering over my head, the longer it will take for me to put this nightmare behind me."

"I was going to wait until a little later but I guess you'll be happy to hear this news now."

"What news?"

Andre walked over to Tyler and sat her down on the couch. "The prosecutor just called before I came downstairs. They worked out a plea agreement with Chantal and her attorney. It's a done deal."

"Are you serious?" Tyler asked as her eyes widened, overjoyed that the case was finally over.

"Yes. Chantal agreed to several years of probation, extensive therapy and to pay a fine. And of course the permanent restraining order will stay in affect."

"Wow, she practically killed me and she walks away with no jail time. Talk about lucky."

"Baby, Chantal's attorney was adamant about no jail time. For that to have happened the case would've had to go to trial. You didn't want to go through months of a long drawn out court case. I definitely didn't want to make a choice about what I would say if I testified."

"Excuse me! Make a choice? What do you mean by that?" Tyler was taken aback by Andre's statement. She instantly stood up from the couch waiting to hear Andre's explanation."

"That was the wrong choice of words. I didn't mean that literally. I'm just glad I wasn't put in the position to have to decide what to do."

"What would you need to decide, whether to save Chantal's ass or stand by your fiancée's side who nearly died trying to protect you?"

"Tyler, you're getting yourself all worked up over nothing. This has nothing to do with Chantal. It's about my daughter and the damage it would've done to her if my testimony would've sent her mother to jail. We discussed this and we both agreed it was best not to pursue it."

"Yeah, but you made it seem that the decision was mine and you had no problem taking that stand and telling the truth whether Chantal went to jail or not. You never gave me the impression that if I had pursued a trial that you were weighing your options as to what you were going to do."

"Baby, listen to me. If you had wanted to take this all the way I would've have supported you no matter what. I mean that. I was torn because I did feel guilty about what happened. A lot of that guilt was because no matter how we feel about Chantal, Melanie loves her mother, and I didn't want the burden of breaking my little girl's heart weighing on my conscious for the rest of my life. I thank you for not putting me in that position, but please believe that this has nothing to do with me trying to protect Chantal. I love you, Tyler, and only you."

Andre lovingly wrapped his arms around Tyler hoping she could feel all the love he had for her. She wanted to believe that what he was saying was true, but part of her still believed that maybe Andre felt some sort of loyalty towards the mother of his child. She wondered if Andre had been put in the position to choose, would he had gone to bat for her, or got selective amnesia for Chantal. Part of her regretted that now with the case resolved she would never have the chance to know.

"I know that you love me, and I love you too. I'm just happy that we can move on with our lives. Hopefully Chantal will get the help that she needs and will not bother us again."

"I believe Chantal has learned her lesson. So now all we have to do is focus on us." Andre held Tyler's chin up and looked in her eyes. He could see there was some sort of hesitation behind her smile but chose not to question it, not wanting to get caught up in a potential argument. He loved her so much and knew only time would give her the security that she needed. "Baby, I have some business I need to handle so I'll give you a call later on," he said, kissing her on the forehead.

"I need to get back to reading this script anyway. Tomorrow is the big day."

"Don't work too hard. I'll see you later on."

The moment Tyler heard the front door shut she went to the kitchen and opened a bottle of champagne. She knew it was a little early to be drinking but she needed something to mellow her out and bubbly always did the trick. She grabbed a glass and headed back to the living room couch with bottle in tow.

Tyler sat back reading her script, and before long she had finished the entire bottle of Dom Perignon. The effect of the alcohol had gone from giving her a buzz to mellowing her out to making her sleepy, which actually relieved her. Her conversation with Andre had left her feeling empty and insecure about their relationship. She knew that he loved her but didn't know how deep his feelings truly ran. Knowing that she was about to start filming a movie, the last thing she wanted to dwell on was her relationship with Andre. If drinking could take the edge off, then why not?

Chantal was making herself very comfortable at Ian's crib. His penthouse apartment had a fabulous view of LA and his taste in furniture was exquisite. She figured this must be his bachelor pad, although he was technically married. She had gone through every part of the place meticulously and didn't see a sign of a child living here or any other woman's belongings. In fact, the place was so spotless it almost appeared that it wasn't lived in. The only area that had any sign of life was the master bedroom and bathroom. The closet was full of men's clothing, which Chantal assumed were Ian's, and the bathroom had the standard toothbrush and other toiletries. The refrigerator was damn near empty, and after a couple of hours had passed Chantal was praying Ian would walk through the door at any moment.

Ring...Ring... Chantal was sitting at the dining room table flipping through a Sports Illustrated magazine she noticed on the kitchen counter when the phone started ringing. She tapped her fingers for a quick second debating on whether or not to answer the phone. "Hello," she answered after the fifth ring.

"Why you answering my phone?" Ian asked in a nondescript tone.

"I figured it was you."

"My number comes up private, so what if it wasn't, then what?"

"I don't know. I guess I would've said I was your cleaning lady and took a message." Chantal knew that was a lie and Ian did too.

"Unless I give you permission, I would appreciate if you don't answer my phone."

"Why the fuck did you call if you didn't want me answering your damn phone?" Chantal was annoyed he was trying to lay the law down when she had just fucked his brains out last night.

"Just to see if you would answer, although I figured you would."

"Oh, so now you trying to play games. I don't advise you to play games with me. But anyway, the real reason I picked up is because I'm starving and you don't have any food in this damn place. Plus I don't have a number on you so I couldn't call to let you know to bring me something back to eat."

"I know that's why I called."

Chantal rolled her eyes thinking to herself that Ian was a piece of work. She was realizing that he was a different kind of trouble that she might not be used to handling. "I see you got tricks with you. So are you going to take my order or what?"

"Actually I was going to tell you that if you look in the drawer next to the phone in the kitchen you will see a black pad. Call the number on the first page and tell them what you want to eat and they'll deliver it to you."

"Is there a menu so I can pick what I want?"

"They'll cook whatever and bring it to you. There's an in-house chef on the premises."

"Damn, that's hot."

"I thought so too. It's one of the reasons I bought the place, little perks like that."

"So when you coming back?" Chantal wanted to know because she was starting to miss him already.

"In a couple of hours."

"Damn, how long is your practice?"

"Practice is over. I just got some things I have to do first before I come back."

"Have you forgotten that I don't have any clothes to put on? I need to go home."

"So you don't want to wait for me?"

"It's not that, I do. But I want to take a shower and get clean, but then to put on clothes I was dancing a storm up in last night would be disgusting."

"I'll tell you what. When you call that number after you order something to eat, tell them to connect you with the personal shopper in the building. Give the lady your size and what you want to wear. She'll come up and give you a selection of stuff to choose from. So when I get back you can be cleaned and dressed, although I prefer you naked."

"Yo, this place is off the chain. A personal shopper. You really know how to make a lady feel at home."

"Well, don't go overboard with the spending, alright?"

"I got you. I'll be waiting for your arrival." When Chantal got off the phone with Ian she immediately called Shari.

"Hello," Shari answered in her cheerful singing voice.

"What's good, honey?"

"Chantal, I've been waiting for yo ass to call me. Your cell phone keep going straight to voice mail."

"My battery died."

"Oh, since you still haven't gotten back home I'm assuming you still lounging over at Ian's place."

"And you know it."

"Well, bitch, spill the 411. You know I've been dying to talk to your scandalous ass."

"Where do I start?"

"With the dick down, that would be nice."

"Yes indeed, it was nice. Girl, you know I haven't fucked in forever. His sex game is official. I was loving it. I was backed up, but honey, I released all my stress. Girl, he wore a condom and I still came three times."

"I knew his fine ass was gonna be the truth."

"No doubt. I can't wait for him to come back so he can put it on me once again."

"Girl, so you chilling up in his crib? How is it?"

"He got a fly ass penthouse. It gotta be the spot he brings his sideline hoes to because it don't look like nobody even be up in here. This place is so official, you call this number and they'll cook anything you want to eat. Since I don't have a change of clothes, Ian also said I could call the personal shopper and pick out something to wear. He definitely got some class with him."

"Chantal, you've lucked up with this one. You better play your cards right."

"Who you telling? I need a replacement for that sorry ass Andre. But I can't front. I'm afraid to get too comfortable because how do you think he's going to react when I tell him who I am?"

"Well then don't tell him yet."

"But I rather he finds out from me first then have someone else fill him in, or worse, he sees my face on the news or in the papers. He would probably kick me right out his front door. I have to tell him now so I can put my own spin on it."

"If anybody's good at putting a spin on something it's you. So I'm confidant you'll find a way to stick around for a little while longer."

"Little! If I have my way I'll be around for *a lot* longer," Chantal stressed the words "a lot".

"I'm not going to keep you. I'm actually about to get dressed because Jalen is taking me out to lunch after he leaves practice."

"He's a cutie. Hopefully things will work out and we'll be double dating in the near future."

"Works for me. If you don't come home again tonight we'll chat tomorrow and keep each other updated about what's going on...later," Shari said hanging up the phone.

After Chantal placed her food order and spoke to the personal shopper, she jumped in the shower and let the hot water cleanse her body. She hadn't felt so alive in so long. She knew it was too soon to be sure, but for the first time she felt optimistic that another man could finally burn out the torch she'd been carrying for Andre for all these years. There was something about Ian that was magnetic. He had charm, confidence and he was also a challenge. She could tell that Ian somewhat liked her, but he gave no indication of how much, which was a turn on. Chantal decided Ian would be her man and that was all she wrote.

Chapter Six

Naughty Girl

Tyler woke up bright and early to prepare for her first day on set. She really wasn't an exercise fanatic but decided a long jog along the beach would rejuvenate her. After drinking the entire bottle of champagne yesterday on an empty stomach she felt groggy and her mind or body still wasn't right when she woke up. So after having a power shake she hit the beach. The cool morning breeze hitting Tyler's face made her feel alive. The peacefulness of it all gave her an opportunity to reflect over a lot of things.

The first person that came to mind was her son, Christian whom she missed terribly. She hadn't seen him since his father, Brian brought him to the hospital after the accident. Tyler felt that with all the media scrutiny and at that time not completely healing it would be best if Christian stayed with his dad for a while. Although she had to beg Brian just to bring Christian to LA since he still detested her so much, seeing his angelic face was exactly what she needed. Now she was about to start filming a movie, and it seemed that the time still wasn't right for Christian to come live with her. Tyler decided one of the first things she would do when she saw William was let him know she needed to schedule two weeks during shooting so she could go to New Jersey and be with her son.

T-Roc was thrilled the day had finally arrived when they would begin filming. He was determined to become a major player in Hollywood and this film was the vehicle to get him started. As T-Roc got dressed he visualized stepping on stage after winning his Oscar, the crowd in awe of his speech and giving him a standing ovation, all the while Tyler is sitting in the audience, cheering her husband on. "The perfect couple they would be indeed," T-Roc said out loud, as he looked at himself in the mirror.

"Good morning," **Chrissie said as she** walked into William's office.

"Good morning to you too. I'm surprised to see you here."

"I know today is Tyler's first day back to work and I was going to head over to the set with you, if you don't mind."

"Of course not. I think it'll be great for you to be there. Tyler needs as much support as possible."

"I feel the same way. She's putting on a good front that everything is fine, but I know Tyler and she's a lot more stressed than she's letting on."

"And being with that lowlife thug Andre isn't of any help. I don't understand what she sees in that man."

"William, I agree that Andre is no good for Tyler, but she loves him. Trying to come between them will only alienate her. We have to try and be supportive of their relationship, or at least pretend to be."

William looked up at Chrissie for the first time and gave her smile. *Pretend* was the key word that he liked. He would pretend to support Tyler's relationship with Andre and at the same time plot to guarantee the end of it.

"Well, let's get out of here. We have a movie to shoot," William said as he grabbed his belongings and they headed out the door.

For the second day in a row, Chantal once again woke up next to Ian and she was in ecstasy. Out of all the men she ever slept with none of them had a body quite as flawless as Ian Addison. His caramel complexion reflected beautifully off the deep cream silk sheets. Chantal spooned herself close to his chest so she could feel his smooth skin. As she snuggled next to him she couldn't figure out for the life of her how Tyler could've ever let him go—or maybe he let her go—Chantal finally decided.

"Damn, I need to get up!" Chantal heard Ian say right when she was about to fall back to sleep in his arms.

"Can't you lay here just a couple hours longer?" she asked seductively.

"Afraid not. I'm leaving today."

"Where are you going?" Chantal asked with a panicked sound in her voice. She caught herself and realized she needed to slow down. She didn't want Ian to think she was already sprung.

"I have a couple of away games, first Indiana then Charlotte."

"Oh." Chantal put her head down and it was obvious she wasn't pleased that Ian had to go.

"Don't look so sad, I'll be back."

As if Chantal had no self-control she asked, "Well can I come with you?" There was awkward silence between them for a moment. Chantal knew she had no business making such a request. If Ian wanted her to come he would've asked, but she couldn't help herself. It had been so long since she had any sort of intimacy with a man and she was more drawn to Ian than she had originally anticipated.

"Chantal, listen."

"No, forget it. I don't know what I was thinking. I have a million things to do anyway. Running behind you at some games isn't exactly productive." As she mumbled on, for the first time Ian saw a slight trace of vulnerability in a woman he originally deemed as completely shallow.

"Let me explain something to you."

"You don't have to explain anything." Chantal felt she'd crossed the line and was embarrassed.

"I want to," he said reassuringly. "I'm not sure if you know this, but I'm married—actually separated. My divorce is almost finalized but my agent, coach, the higher ups, attorney, just everybody wants me to somewhat keep a low profile until my divorce is a done deal. Which means traveling with me and going to the games isn't possible right now."

"I understand."

"Are you sure?"

"Yes, you don't need anything to make you look bad in the media or to make your soon to be ex-wife more upset than I'm sure she already is."

"Pretty much."

"If you don't mind me asking, what happened between the two of you that led to the separation?"

"Honestly, I'm not in love with her, never was. Unlike most men in the league who aren't in love with their wives but decide to stay, I bounced."

"If you weren't in love with her, why did you marry her in the first place?"

"When you reach a certain status in the league they put so much pressure on you to settle down and get married. They want you to have this ideal life for endorsement deals and all that other bullshit. When my girl got pregnant I figured fuck it, I'll go head and marry her. She wasn't going to stop me from doing what I wanted to do so I thought it wouldn't be that bad. But the only thing worse than having a woman nag you is having one you're not in love with nag you. I couldn't take it no more. It got to the point that I dreaded going home after games and listening to her trying to boss me in my own house. My father always told me, if you not running your house then you need to get out of it, so that's what I did."

"So how is she taking it?"

"On the real, she's sick about it. She figured she'd be living the life of a NBA superstar's wife forever. But with the pre-nup she signed, that's out of the question. She's not a bad chick and honestly it's not her fault I'm not in love with her. Since women are harder to get rid of than herpes, I figured I throw her something extra in the settlement so we can end this on a decent note. She is the mother of my child so I'll have to deal with her for a very long time."

Chantal wasn't sure if the burning sensation in her chest was from the repulsion she had for what Ian just admitted or because his blatant honesty was making her even more attracted to him. She had to admit to herself that when a woman finds a great catch like an Ian Addison or Andre Jackson they don't want to let them go. They're willing to walk through fire to hold on. I mean, what woman doesn't want to lay back and luxuriate and have her every materialistic need met? But for Ian to throw it up in her face and to acknowledge it as fact felt like a stinging slap.

"I hope everything works out the way that you want it to."

The iciness in Chantal's voice was transparent. Ian knew that something he said offended her but he didn't care. She asked for the truth and he gave it to her. "So will I see you when I get back?"

"I'm not sure if you'll want to."

Ian eyed her quizzically not understanding why she'd made such a statement. "What the hell does that mean?"

Chantal figured since Ian revealed what was going on in his personal life, she should do the same. Eventually he would find out about her past and Chantal decided to get it out in the open now so she could try to forget about Ian Addison if he decided to kick her to the curb after her revelation. "Since we're being honest, I have a few secrets I need to confide to you."

When Tyler arrived on set she was greeted by her best friend and publicist, Chrissie. She had to admit she was pleasantly surprised to see her. Tyler had bubbles in her stomach due to her nervousness, and having Chrissie there for support was exactly what she needed.

"Tyler, you look great!" Chrissie beamed.

"Thanks, I had a wonderful morning. I jogged along the beach and I feel incredible. It's amazing what fresh air and exercise can do for the mind and body. I think I might make it a permanent ritual in my life."

"Well, you already know that I believe exercising is essential for productivity so I think that's a great idea."

"I knew you would. But seriously, it really did help me to get my mind focused. Speaking of focusing, I have to speak to William. There is something I need to discuss with him."

"Here I am," William said as he walked up behind Chrissie and Tyler.

Tyler had been so caught up in telling the story of her new found love for jogging she hadn't noticed William talking to a gentleman just a few feet away. "Hi," she said, giving William a hug.

"Tyler, you look beautiful." And she did. Tyler had her jet black wavy hair going back in a long French braid. Her skin had a radiant glow to it and the clear gloss highlighted her full seductive lips.

"Thank you, Mr. Donovan," she said playfully.

"Before we get to what you need to discuss with me, once again congratulations on your movie, 'Angel' opening number one at the box office. I'm so proud of you. You're on your way to being a superstar."

"You're so sweet, and thank you for all the flowers you had delivered this morning. When I got back from jogging I thought I stepped in a flower shop instead of my living room."

"You deserved it," William said, feeling proud of his protégé. "So what do you need to discuss?"

"Within the next month I want to go to New Jersey and spend a couple of weeks with Christian. I miss him so much."

"Say no more. That's no problem. We actually have to film in New York for a month."

"Really? I had no idea. That's wonderful!"

"Yeah, so we can sit down sometime this week and I'll let you know the exact date we're leaving so you can do whatever scheduling preparation you'll need."

"You're the best. Thanks so much."

"Anything for you." William gave Tyler a kiss on the cheek. "Chrissie, show Tyler to her trailer. We'll all meet back out here in about twenty minutes. See you soon."

"Has T-Roc gotten here yet?" Tyler asked as she and Chrissie walked towards her trailer.

"Yeah, I saw him briefly about fifteen minutes ago. He was talking to William before he went to his trailer. Are you uneasy about working with him?"

"A little bit. But I'm sure once I get my feet wet it'll be business as usual."

58

"Chrissie, can I speak to you for a second?" William's assistant yelled out from a distance."

"What is it now?" Chrissie sighed to Tyler under her breath.

"Go ahead, I'll be fine. I need to go in my trailer and unwind for a minute anyway. I'll see you shortly."

"Okay, darling."

Chrissie walked off in the direction of William's assistant and Tyler headed up the stairs towards her trailer. When Tyler opened the door all anyone heard was the ear piercing noise from her screams.

"What the hell is going on?" William shouted as he came out of the back room.

Even over the music T-Roc had blasting in his trailer he heard the gut wrenching cries. He hurried out of his trailer anxious to see where the screams were coming from. When he came outside, from a short distance he saw Tyler standing in front of her door with a horrified look on her face. Everyone was calling her name as they ran to her aid but it was as if she was frozen with fear.

T-Roc reached Tyler at the same time as William and the inside of her trailer looked like a bad rendition of a "Saw" horror flick. There were dozens of bouquets of dead black roses, and what looked to be blood splattered over her walls, and on the mirror was written, *You Will Die, Bitch.* In the corner there was a bucket of mutilated rats, and they realized where the blood came from. Tyler was shaking uncontrollably, and while William was calling security and clearing the area, T-Roc held Tyler and she practically melted in his arms.

"Who could've done this?" was all Tyler kept saying over and over again as her voice shivered.

"I don't know, but we will find out and I promise they'll pay," T-Roc said as he stroked her hair. T-Roc was finally able to calm her down and escorted her to his trailer while security waited for the police to come.

Tyler could hear William yelling and screaming at the top of his lungs. William was normally in control and very calm, but when he lost his temper he became a beast and right now he was furious. He knew there was no way Tyler would be ready to work today and he couldn't blame her. One thing William hated was wasting time and money.

"Could you get me something to drink?" Tyler asked when she sat down on the couch in T-Roc's trailer. T-Roc went to his mini refrigerator and got bottled water and handed it to her. "No, I mean something stronger, like champagne, wine or any liquor."

"Sorry, I don't have any." After Tyler's request T-Roc couldn't help but reflect on the brief time they dated how Tyler always turned to alcohol when the pressure became too much. During that time he had also introduced her to some pills to make her feel better, but T-Roc doubted she was using any narcotics.

"Don't worry about it. I need to call Andre." Tyler's hands were shaking as she struggled to find her cell inside her purse. She finally found the tiny phone and called him. "Fuck, it keeps going straight to voice mail."

"Calm down, it'll be okay."

"Someone wants me dead! Did you see that? There were dead rats in my trailer with blood everywhere. What type of sick monster would do such a thing? T-Roc, I can't deal with this right now. First Chantal, now this. I'm going to go crazy!"

Tyler was now pacing back and forth in the spacious trailer when William barged in. "Tyler, are you okay."

"What the hell do you think? There's some psycho out there who wants me dead. How did the monster get in my trailer and do all that without anyone noticing? I don't feel safe."

"I know. I'm trying to figure that out right now. But from this day forward there will be two security guards posted outside the door of your new trailer. There will be extra security on the entire set. It being the first day on set, everybody was lax, but that will never happen again. The police are searching the trailer thoroughly for any type of clues as to who did this."

"I have to get out of here."

William gently grabbed Tyler by both her arms. He calmed himself because he knew one of them had to be in control. He spoke in a composed tone. "Tyler, go home and get some rest. But I need you to be strong and pull it together so we can start production tomorrow. It's important that you're here. I need you." He lifted Tyler's face so he could look her directly in the eyes. William felt he knew Tyler better than anyone and how to get through to her. "Do you understand me? I need you to pull it together. You're on your way to becoming a major superstar and people are going to come at you in all directions. Stalkers, neurotic fans and people who are just obsessed with you, but I'll protect you for now on, but you have to trust me. This will never happen again. I'm so sorry."

Tyler seemed to break free from the traumatized world she was stuck in. "I'll be here tomorrow ready to work. I promise."

"That's my girl. Now you go home. I'll call you later on to make sure you're okay." William kissed Tyler on the forehead and nodded his head at T-Roc and left.

T-Roc was impressed by how William handled Tyler. They definitely had a connection and it was obvious Tyler had a great deal of respect for him. "I'll walk you to your car."

"Thank you, I definitely don't want to be alone." Tyler grabbed her purse and they walked to the parking lot.

When they reached her car, to further add to Tyler's grief the same person that sabotaged her trailer flattened all four tires and left a single black rose on her windshield. If it wasn't for T-Roc being by her side Tyler had no doubt that she would've collapsed right there on the spot.

"So what dirty little secrets do you need to get off your chest?" Ian said with a chuckle. He figured whatever Chantal had to say wasn't that serious and she was only trying to be dramatic since she didn't take too kindly to his frankness regarding his relationship with his wife.

"Did you hear the story about the would be bride who tried to run over the would be groom?" Ian looked up at the ceiling trying to recall if he had heard such a story. He wasn't really a news person so nothing was popping up until Chantal said, "But ended up hitting the actress Tyler Blake instead?"

"You're not the psycho bride that damn neared killed Tyler?" he questioned with total shock in his voice.

Chantal could tell by the tone in his question that it was almost as if he was taking it personally. "Do you know Tyler?" Chantal asked although she knew that he did but wanted to get an exact read on his feelings towards Tyler before she went on with her confession.

"Yes, we dated a long time ago."

"Oh, I didn't know you dated Tyler," she lied and said, "Was it serious?"

"Very serious. Now back to you. Are you the woman that almost killed her?"

Chantal swallowed hard, instantly regretting that she ever decided to share her sordid past. Originally she was heated with his egotistical attitude about his wife and divorce but now felt that she had a momentary lapse in judgment with her decision to come clean. She felt certain that Ian would show her the front door, maybe even grab her and literally throw her out of it. "Yes, I'm the one. I honestly didn't mean to hit her. I only wanted to hurt my fiancé at the time, Andre. But Tyler pushed him out the way trying to save his life and I hit her instead."

"Un-fucking believable! Out of all the women in LA the one woman I decide to go home with from the club would be certifiable. Not only that, you hit the woman I used to be in a relationship with. What are the odds in that?"

Chantal knew exactly what those odds were since she made it her mission the moment he walked in that club for him to be with her, knowing full well he had been in a relationship with Tyler. "Some things are meant to be."

"Chantal, give me a break. I doubt what we have is meant to be."

"I guess it's just me then because I thought we had a connection."

"Connecting with someone physically and being 'meant to be' are two entirely different things. But you know what is funny? When I compared your feisty attitude with my ex, I was talking about Tyler."

Chantal felt nauseated. She always thought she and Tyler were on opposite sides of the spectrum when it came to personality traits. Chantal assumed that was one of the reasons Andre chose Tyler because she was a fragile, little flower. To think that she could spit fire just like her, but Andre still wanting Tyler just added insult to injury. "So, Tyler is feisty. I had no idea."

"Yeah, most people don't know it unless you date her. She has this whole angelic thing going on, but trust me, she is something else."

Chantal could tell that they definitely had a lot of history and whatever skeletons they shared he wasn't ready to reveal. "Listen, Ian, I understand if you're reluctant about dating me but I wish you wouldn't be so quick to judge me. I made a horrible mistake but Andre had driven me to the point that I felt I was losing my mind. He's the father of my daughter and the man I believed I would spend the rest of my life with. For him to dump me on the day of our wedding was just too much for me, and then to find him cozying up to another woman, I was overwhelmed. I know that isn't an excuse and you're probably thinking I'm some crazy broad and I'll flip out like that on you too, but trust me, that was a once in a lifetime experience."

"Aren't you going to trial or to jail or something anyway?"

"Luckily I had an excellent attorney and he worked out a plea agreement for me and I won't be getting any jail time, just probation and community service."

"Damn, who the fuck is your attorney?"

"Mitchell Stern."

"Mitchell. That's my man. Yeah, he's definitely a miracle worker. Well, I'm happy everything worked out for you and I hope you get it together, mentally I mean, so nothing like this ever happens again."

"I will be getting therapy, but I'm not crazy, Ian. Is it so hard to believe that maybe a man can make you lose your mind for a moment?"

"No, but not every woman tries to run him over either."

"I guess that means I won't be seeing you when you get back from Charlotte."

"I don't think it's a good idea."

Chantal slowly gathered her belongings hoping Ian would change his mind. But after she spent forty-five minutes pretending to look for her shoe that was clearly visible under the chair, she accepted the fact it was a lost cause.

Ian called downstairs for the car service and gave her a slight wave goodbye. He didn't even walk her to the door. So much for it being meant to be.

Chapter Seven

Fall to Pieces

When T-Roc drove Tyler home, she insisted he come in because no one was there and she didn't want to be alone. Before T-Roc even took a seat, Tyler had disappeared and shortly after reappeared with a bottle of champagne in one hand and a glass in the other. "I would offer you some but one of us needs to be completely sober just in case that crazy animal decides to show up at my front door."

"Tyler, no one is going to show up here. Plus, this place is gated with a security guard right up front. And there are cameras everywhere. You're safe here."

"I'm glad you're so confident because I'm a nervous wreck."

T-Roc took note that Tyler was already on her second glass of champagne and he hadn't even been there for ten minutes. "I know you're stressed, but maybe you should ease up on the champagne."

"I don't think so. This is the only thing that's going to calm my nerves."

It amazed T-Roc that after all this time Tyler still had the same weaknesses. He knew exactly how he would manipulate her to be back in his bed.

"Baby, I came home as soon as I got your message," Andre belted as he ran towards Tyler, interrupting T-Roc's scheming thoughts.

"Where were you? I kept calling your cell and it was going straight to voice mail."

"I was in the recording studio and I wasn't getting any reception. I should've given you the number to where I was going to be. I'm so sorry."

"Don't worry, I'm just glad your home."

Andre held Tyler for a minute and quickly realized they weren't alone. "What are you doing here?" he growled at T-Roc.

"Baby, T-Roc walked me to my car, and when we got there all the tires were flat and the psycho left a single black rose. He was kind enough to give me a ride home."

"Thanks, but you can go now, I'm here."

"Yeah, it's too bad you weren't there when she really needed you, but I forgot you were in the studio," T-Roc said mockingly.

"What the fuck do you mean by that?"

"Both of you, please stop! I don't need this right now. T-Roc, thanks for the ride and I'll see you tomorrow."

"No problem. Call me if you need me."

"Don't count on that call. Tyler won't be needing you for nothing." Andre and T-Roc gave each other the hooligan stare-down as T-Roc left. "Baby, I know you're not going back to work tomorrow!"

"Andre, I have to."

"No you don't. You can stay right here at home and relax."

"We already missed today and William needs me."

"Fuck William! You know I don't care about his snake ass anyway."

"He isn't a snake, Andre," Tyler said, releasing herself from Andre's grasp as she reached for the champagne bottle to refill her glass.

"Why you defending that cat? He couldn't even protect you on his own movie set. How in the fuck did someone get in your trailer and do all that foul shit and didn't nobody notice?"

"I asked William the same question. It was the first day and security was slack. He promised it would never happen again. Baby, there is no way you can be more frustrated than me, but I can't let whoever this asshole is keep me from working."

Andre huffed loudly as he became more frustrated with Tyler's reasoning. "If you insist on going back to work, then let me have some of my security men drive you to and from work and also stay on the set with you."

"That's fine. I would like that anyway."

"Good. I feel a little better. Now if only I could get rid of that slick ass snake, T-Roc."

"Stop. He isn't all that bad."

"Yeah, there just ain't nothing good about him." Andre went on for another ten minutes about his dislike for T-Roc and William. But Andre might as well been talking to the wall because while he was venting, Tyler had finished her bottle and was on her way to the kitchen for number two.

Chantal and Shari sat in the Chateau Marmont in Hollywood having drinks and discussing men. Shari was actually relieved that Chantal was now complaining about a guy other than Andre. That was a day she never saw coming. "So yeah, girl, Mr. Ian Addison kicked me to the curb. He was so nonchalant about it too. I must be losing my touch."

"Chantal, it doesn't have anything to do with you losing your touch. I mean you did tell him you tried to run over your ex fiancée. That's a hard pill to swallow for any man."

"I know, but it seemed as if he was more bothered that I hit Tyler."

"What you mean, like he still got feelings for her or something?"

"Something is still there. He also got a lot of dirt on that chick that I'm dying to know about, but I guess I'll never find out now."

"What would you do with the information anyway, run and tell Andre, for what so he'll come back to you?"

"Hell no. Believe it or not, I don't want Andre back. Any man that can drive me that crazy I don't need them in my life. But I would like to knock his little princess, Tyler Blake off of her pedestal. He acts like she is so perfect. I know that hussy got skeletons just like the rest of us. Maybe if Andre saw that he wouldn't be so hard on me."

"I feel you, but with Ian out of your life there's no way to uncover Tyler's hidden secrets."

"One monkey ain't never stopped a show. I'll get what I need on Tyler whether it be by rapping or clapping."

"Girl, you better stop ripping off Jay-Z lines," Shari laughed.

"I need a Tyler break...so what's up with you and Jalen?"

"We've been out a couple of times and I'm digging him. I know he's young with extra long paper so he probably ain't trying to settle down, but he got a laid back style that's sexy as shit."

"You never know, them young cats be trying to settle down quick sometimes, trying to prove they grown and shit. But whatever you do, don't drop no seed for him unless he wife you first. And I don't mean have no fake ass long engagement like La La and Carmelo Anthony and play pretend house. You wait for that cat to walk you down the aisle and the vows have been exchanged."

"Damn, Chantal, what, you a psychic? You talking like me and Jalen engaged and about to get married. We haven't even been dating a month yet."

"I know, but I just have a feeling that your spaceship may have finally landed."

"That would be some shit if it did. Jalen paper is super long." While Shari was talking, Chantal noticed a middle-aged white gentleman staring at them, and then he stood up and started walking towards their direction.

"Here comes some clown. I hope he don't think we some high priced call girls and we are going to offer him some two for one special."

"Hi, ladies, my name is Rupert Douglas," The man extended his hand and Chantal was about to rebuff him but then he said, "Aren't you Chantal Morgan?"

"How do you know my name?" Chantal was curious to know.

"I saw you on Larry King with your attorney. I thought you handled yourself beautifully."

"Oh, thanks," Chantal said blandly. She was ready to put that whole psycho bride scandal behind her, especially after losing Ian over it.

"My, dear, you should sound a lot more cheerful. I have a guaranteed way for you to become a star overnight and a very wealthy young woman."

"Star" and "wealthy" in the same sentence sparked Chantal's interest. "How do plan to do that?"

"Does a seven figure book deal interest you?"

After T-Roc left Tyler's house he headed back over to the movie set. He wanted to see if the police made any leeway to finding out who was responsible for the threat against Tyler. When he pulled up in the parking lot he noticed Chrissie walking towards her car. T-Roc rushed to get out so he could catch her before she pulled off.

"Chrissie, wait up," T-Roc yelled out.

Chrissie turned around and to her delight, saw it was T-Roc. "Hi, what's going on? I wanted to speak with you earlier but you were busy and then that unfortunate fiasco with Tyler happened. I miss you. You haven't returned any of my phone calls," she added.

"It's been hectic, you know, preparing for the movie and maintaining all the other projects I have going on."

"I understand, but I would love if you could make some time for me. You know, for old time's sake," Chrissie said flirtatiously.

"Chrissie, I'm flattered but we agreed that I wasn't any good for you in a romantic way and we should just be friends, remember?"

"I do, but what could it hurt for us to get together occasionally? You can't deny how incredible our lovemaking was together."

"No doubt, but I still believe you deserve someone much better than me. I care about you and our friendship is too valuable for me to do anything to mess it up." T-Roc was laying it on thick because his eyes were on the prize, which was Tyler. He didn't need to start up a sexual relationship with Chrissie again and ruin his chances with Tyler.

"T-Roc, you're incredibly noble. I can't lie and say I'm not disappointed with your decision, but at the same time I appreciate your concern for me."

T-Roc gently rubbed the side of Chrissie's cheek. "You're an amazing woman, Chrissie, and you're going to make someone a very lucky man. If only I was worthy it could be me, but I'm not, so let's not dwell on that."

Chrissie blushed and T-Roc knew he had her eating out the palm of his hand. She truly fit the description of a dumb blonde. With her flowing sun-kissed locks and California girl tanned physique, her gullible personality was truly her most appealing attribute to T-Roc. She was a sucker for him and he planned on using it to his advantage. "But enough about what I wish we could've had. Do the cops have a lead on who destroyed Tyler's trailer?"

"Not yet, but you know William will get to the bottom of it. Poor Tyler, it seems she has one tragedy after another."

"Seven figure book deal! That sounds tasty indeed, but the thing is I don't write."

"My delectable Chantal," he said as he patted Chantal's shoulder.

Shari and Chantal both looked at each other and they knew exactly what the other one was thinking. This man was getting way too comfortable, as if he and Chantal went way back. Chantal used her right hand to brush his hand off.

"I apologize. When I'm excited about a new idea I get a little touchy. But actually, this isn't a new idea. I got it when I first saw you on television. I even left several messages for your attorney trying to get a hold of you but he never returned my calls. Then so my luck, here you are. I guess when things are meant to be they happen."

Those words sounded familiar to Chantal and she remembered that was the line she tried to use on Ian but he wasn't falling for it. But for some reason it sounded awfully nice coming out of Rupert's mouth. "So, Rupert, what did you say you did again?"

"Glad you asked. I'm an agent, but not just any agent. I'm the biggest literary agent on the West Coast—some might say both coasts."

Rupert pulled out his business card and handed one to Chantal and Shari as he winked his eye. Both ladies thought it looked official but they were still suspect of the flamboyantly dressed man. Then some snobby looking older white lady wearing designer labels Chantal couldn't even pronounce and enough ice to start her own diamond outlet gave him the two fake kisses on each cheek and said, "Rupert, you did wonders for my niece. New York Times bestseller! Not even I imagined that. I'll call you. We'll do lunch soon. Bye."

"Rupert, why don't you have a seat? The drinks are on me," Chantal said as she quickly warmed up to him.

"But of course. We have so much to discuss."

"I do want to hear what you have to say, but I must tell you I barely passed English in high school."

Rupert began laughing and shaking his head as if what Chantal told him was the funniest joke of the year. The two women were still puzzled by the man but knew he was the real deal so they let it slide.

"I love that realness about you. That alone will sell us another hundred thousand copies of your book. But seriously, let me school you on a few things."

"School me," Chantal said now laughing just like Rupert was a second ago. "Let me find out you got some gangsta with you."

"Oh my dear, if getting money is what you define as gangsta, then arrest me now because I'm guilty."

Chantal was beginning to like Rupert's style more and more.

"Now as I was saying, most celebrities and other so called authors who pen tell all's aren't writers. They have either ghost writers or co-writers who do all the work. They couldn't put a storyline together to save their lives. But does the publisher really care? No, of course not. Their only concern is how many books they'll sell. I guarantee you, with your story this will be a number one bestseller—not two, not three—but number one!"

Rupert paused and put his hands up above his head as if reading a headline from a Times Square billboard. "Beautiful would be bride runs over Hollywood starlet. It doesn't get any better than that. I see movie written all over it. Wouldn't it be a twist if Tyler Blake played your part on the big screen? And how about winning her first Oscar doing it? I love this business." Rupert bellowed as he bit down on his bottom lip. The guy was definitely 'special'.

"So you really think you can get me a seven figure deal?" Chantal cut right to it because the money was the only thing on her mind.

"*Think* isn't a word I use. I *know* I can. And that's just for the book deal. We're not talking about speaking engagements and all the other opportunities that will come your way."

"Speaking engagements; I don't have time to be speaking to no damn body."

"Kitten, when you see the amount on those checks rolling in you'll have your lovely friend over there," he pointed towards Shari, "Booking them for you. That's how excited you'll be."

"So what's the next step? I'm ready to make that money."

"I'll send you over an agent agreement, have your attorney look it over, and once you give it back to me signed, I'll start a bidding war that even Senator Hillary Clinton would respect."

"Alright, Rupert, you talk a big game. I'll give you that."

"Darling, if it's not big then I don't do it." Rupert gave his signature wink and Chantal had no doubt that he would deliver.

When Tyler woke up she was too tired to go for her morning run. After finishing off her second bottle of champagne before going to bed her body was weak, but she felt she had no other choice.

After begging Andre to stay with her he explained that he had a session in the studio that he needed to finish up. He left a security guard to watch over her, but Tyler still felt alone. She was so lonely that she almost gave in to the urge to call T-Roc for comfort but reasoned that wasn't a good idea. So instead she opted for some champagne to put her in a comatose state of mind. But now Tyler needed something to boost her energy. She located a couple of Stackers in her drawer, but she hated taking them because although they did give her a major pick me up, her stomach also got queasy. But she was desperate. She knew it was imperative she be on point today so she went downstairs, made her power shake and swallowed her Stacker.

"Ms. Blake, what time would you like to leave?" the burly security guard asked.

"I'll be ready in about an hour."

"That's fine. I'll be waiting. Just let me know when you're ready."

"Thanks. By the way, do you know what time Andre left this morning?"

"He didn't come home. He had an all-nighter at the studio. He called and checked up on you a few times but you were asleep."

Tyler couldn't help but feel neglected. She knew Andre had left her protected but she wanted to fall asleep and wake up feeling secure in his arms. All she had was a cold bed and an empty bottle to snuggle up with.

She picked up the phone and called Andre, first on his cell and of course it went straight to voice mail. She then called him at the studio, but no one was picking up. It was early and Tyler figured he was still sleep, but that didn't help ease her displeasure.

After Tyler showered and dressed she got in the back of the SUV and headed over to the movie set. She kept looking at her phone hoping that Andre would call. She needed to hear his voice so he could reassure her that everything would be okay. Since she woke up, she had been replaying the horrific images of dead rats and splattered blood over again in her head. She desperately wanted to get the images out of her mind but she couldn't. They were absorbing her every thought.

When they pulled up to the front entrance, Tyler instantly noticed all the extra security that William put in place, and that made her feel somewhat better. Besides that, she also had the two security guards that Andre put in place. When she walked up both William and Chrissie were there to greet her.

"Hi, guys. I'm so happy to see both of you."

"I'm so proud of you. I know this must be difficult but I knew you wouldn't let me down." William hugged Tyler and he was right, Tyler felt a great sense of obligation to William and she wouldn't let him down.

"We have a new trailer set up for you and I checked it myself. It's perfect. You have two guards at your door and I see you brought along some extra beef. You might be a little over protected."

"I'm starting to feel that way, but I need that right now."

"Everything will be fine. Go to your trailer relax for a second. Then we'll get you in hair and makeup so we can get things started." William gave Tyler a playful massage on her shoulder trying to keep her spirit upbeat. He knew they needed to stay on schedule, but he also wanted Tyler to feel comfortable.

Chrissie walked Tyler to her trailer and stayed for a few minutes trying to put her at ease. But with so much protection Tyler had no problem letting Chrissie leave so she could get her own work done. Tyler sat down and looked over the morning schedule so she could see exactly what William had planned for them. All but one of her scenes was with T-Roc, which was to be expected.

As Tyler went through a couple of minor revisions that were made to the script she heard a knock at her door. "Yes, what is it?"

"You have a visitor, but you locked the door," the security guard posted outside her trailer said.

"Well who is it?" Tyler wasn't sure if she wanted to see anybody right now.

"T-Roc."

"Oh, here I come." That was one person Tyler was looking forward to seeing. "Come on in." Tyler unlocked and opened the door.

"Wow, it's like Fort Knox out there."

"I know, right. At least that maniac can't get to me now."

"I wasn't going to let that happen anyway."

"T-Roc, you're so sweet."

"I just don't want anything to happen to you. You were pretty shaken up when I left you yesterday. Were you able to get some sleep last night?"

"Finally, after I finished my second bottle of champagne."

"That will no doubt make you pass out, but I'm sure Andre tucked you in bed."

"Actually Andre had to go back to the studio last night, so technically my bottle tucked me in. I mean he did leave security with me but I just got a little restless and needed something to put me to sleep."

"You don't have to defend Andre. I can't believe he left you alone last night."

"I said I had security," Tyler snapped, becoming defensive.

"You know what I mean by 'alone'. Andre should've been there for you. He saw how distraught you were. Well at least you woke up with him by your side." T-Roc saw Tyler look down at the floor and then away without saying anything. "Andre did come home last night?"

"He got caught up at the studio. You know how those things go."

T-Roc couldn't believe how easy Andre was going to make it for him to steal his girl. He was already neglecting Tyler as if they had been married for over ten years. T-Roc knew what his problem was. Andre was used to dealing with women like Chantal who would put up with any bullshit he threw their way because he was the best they dreamed of ever getting. Because of that, when a real jewel like Tyler comes along, he doesn't even know how to appreciate her. But T-Roc figured what was Andre's loss would be his gain.

"Tyler, I'm not going to lecture you about your relationship with Andre because that's the man you love and have chosen to be with, but if you ever need to talk I'm here for you."

Tyler was surprised by T-Roc's approach. She knew he would start bashing Andre and giving her the riot act for accepting his treatment, but she got none of that from him. So instead of using her energy defending Andre, she was now left with questioning herself as to why she was tolerating how Andre was treating her, which was exactly what T-Roc was trying to accomplish. "I appreciate that. I was actually tempted to call you last night but changed my mind. I knew you were probably busy anyway."

"I'm never too busy for you. No matter what's happened in the past, I always have your best interest at heart." While T-Roc was talking he noticed Tyler holding her stomach so he asked, "Are you feeling okay?"

"If it isn't one thing it's another."

"You're not pregnant are you?" T-Roc never liked the word "no" coming from a woman, but this was one time he was praying that would be the answer to his question.

"No. I woke up this morning with absolutely no energy so I took a Stacker, and now my stomach is so upset."

"Tyler, you shouldn't fuck with those Stackers. They aren't good for you. If you need something to give you a boost, I have some all natural pills that will do the trick."

"You mean like those pills you used to give me before, that I called dolls," Tyler said with a smirk.

"Yeah, those."

"I'll keep that in mind. Hopefully I'll pull it together and I won't need the pills or alcohol. I think two bottles of champagne in one day is a bit too much."

"I would recommend you slow down."

"I know, but it's so hard. It's crazy because ever since I was a little girl all I did was dream of being a movie star. Never did I realize that so many other things come along with that. Between all the tabloids, media scrutiny, then getting hit by a car, and now some crazy person out there who wants me dead, I didn't sign up for all of this. I just wanted to act and be loved by adoring fans. To have people tell me how wonderful I am, what a great actress I am, and how beautiful I am. That all sounds so superficial but it's the truth. I'm starting to feel as if I'm losing myself. It seems one day I was the rising star of Hollywood and now I can't pick up a newspaper or a magazine without my face being splattered across it. It's all happening so fast and I just wish I could push a button to slow it down."

T-Roc was at a loss for words. For the very first time he could see clearly that this was real. Bit by bit, Tyler was falling apart. "Tyler, don't," T-Roc said as he saw her pulling out a container that he assumed was alcohol.

"I just need a small glass to get me through the morning. I'll be fine."

"I'm going to get you through this. I promise I won't let anything happen to you." T-Roc meant every word. No matter how conniving and cruel T-Roc could be, he truly had a soft spot for Tyler. He always felt the need to save her.

Chapter Eight

Whispers in Bed

When Tyler arrived home from being on the movie set all day she was hoping Andre would be there waiting with open arms. But once again she came home to an empty place with nothing but her bodyguard to keep her company. She only spoke to Andre briefly during the day when he called to check on her. It seemed lately he had no time for Tyler, and she was feeling isolated from the man that she loved.

Although Tyler was craving for a drink, she opted to take a long hot bath instead. She was feeling groggy all day while working and couldn't afford to have another day like that. The combination of the hot bath and Sade's greatest hits playing on the CD player did calm her nerves. She began closing her eyes and falling into a deep sleep until she was awakened by the touch of the softest lips on her neck.

"Baby, I've missed you," Andre whispered in her ear. Tyler turned her head to face his and just began letting her ardent kisses speak for her. Andre lifted her out the tub and Tyler's body went limp in his arms, freeing her of all the tension that had been building up inside her. He laid Tyler down on the bed and admired her still damp body. The water that lightly layered her body highlighted every curve on her butterscotch complexion.

"Andre, please make love to me," Tyler purred, yearning for his touch. Having Andre inside of her was what she needed to feel safe again.

"Shh!" he gestured as he put his finger over Tyler's open mouth. "I just want to take a moment and be in awe of my precious lady. I can't wait for the day I can say 'my wife'." Andre took his hand and gently caressed the outline of Tyler's body. He took his time exploring every curve, appreciating what he had.

Tyler was becoming eager. She desperately needed to be close to Andre. She was tempted to reach up and rip off his clothes but instead tried to remain patient. But finally Andre began to undress, exposing this powerful cocoa colored body. The muscles in his arms flexed as he lifted his thermal shirt over his head and Tyler couldn't wait for those arms to be wrapped around her body as Andre thrust in and out of her.

Tyler would've been fine if Andre skipped the foreplay but he wanted to satisfy her in every way. He lifted one leg a time and sprinkled each with kisses, slowly making his way up to his heaven. He used the tip of his tongue to glide back and forth, giving her clitoris a tingling sensation.

Tyler latched on to the bedpost as her hips began to wind to the beat of Andre's tongue. Right when she was at the point of reaching her climax, Andre pulled his tongue out and put his manhood in. All Tyler could do was let out a scream of passion as she finally got what she'd been craving for.

Chantal and Shari were still babbling on about their conversation with Rupert Douglass as they sat on the couch in Chantal's apartment. "So you think he can deliver what he promised?" Chantal asked Shari, just wanting her best friend to reaffirm what she already believed to be true.

"Girl, you know that flaming white boy was official. He is definitely about his paper, and if he's eating you're eating. He seem a little greedy to me so he is gonna make sure ya are eating real good. I'm talking filet mignon, lobster tail, all that tasty shit. The real question is if you're ready to put all your business out there on front street like that. You saw how everybody dogged that Superhead chick out. And let's not forget Nas baby mama, calling herself the Helen of Troy of hip-hop. These hoes out here kill me. Pretty soon every groupie bitch is going to drop a book."

"Yeah, but them silly broads was running around talking about all the dick they sucked and then spinning it as a cautionary tale. That's bullshit! Them chicks need to have kept it real and just said they were trying to get that loot anyway possible, then they could've told everybody to kiss they ass on those interviews. You can't play good girl/bad girl at the same time. You need to pick a team and stick to it. When I come out with my book I'm being straight up with people. I was basically a money getting hooker trying to score a rich man to make me his housewife. Unfortunately I ended up behind a wheel of a Benz knocking over Tyler Blake in the process. Fuck it! People are either going to cheer for me or hate me, but regardless, I'll be laughing all the way to the bank."

"You have a point there. But you know Andre is going to be pissed as shit."

"Who gives a fuck? His dumb ass still got a restraining order against me in effect. I'm the mother of his child, for heaven's sake. What, we never going to be in a room together again?"

"It's just going to take time. I mean damn, you did try to kill him."

"I blacked out for a minute, that's all. Andre knows that I don't stay mad that long over nothing. It's all love."

"Girl, you just silly as shit, that's all. Maybe once you start your therapy sessions he'll see you're serious about making things right and he'll come around."

"I can't really worry about that right now. I'm too interested in this book deal. Rupert is going to have the agent agreement delivered to me tomorrow and I'm sending them right over to Mitchell so I can get this party started." As Chantal was continuing to talk, they both heard her cell phone ringing.

"Maybe that's Rupert right now," Shari said with a snicker.

Chantal didn't recognize the number but picked up anyway. "Hello."

"You got a minute?"

"That depends on who it's for," Chantal said, not recognizing the voice on the other end.

"It's Ian. You got a minute for me?"

Chantal's eyes widened with excitement. She covered her mouth, and then started using the same hand to point to her cell phone as she mouthed to Shari that it was Ian on the phone.

Shari then became excited too because she couldn't believe that Chantal was behaving like a love struck teenager who was getting asked to the spring dance.

"I'm surprised to hear from you," she said coyly.

"I know, but it's been a few days and you've been on my mind."

"Really," she said, not sounding as if she totally believed him.

"Yeah, for real. I'll be back tomorrow and I was hoping I could see you."

"Uhmm hmm, I would like that."

"Okay, so I'll call you sometime tomorrow afternoon."

When Ian hung up the phone he sat back in the bed at the hotel room he was staying in. He was still deciphering why he decided to see Chantal again. After her little confession he really thought it best to leave her the fuck alone. The last thing he wanted to be bothered with was a woman with a lot of drama. He knew if he ever really kicked it with Chantal like that, the press would have a field day, and although Ian loved being a NBA superstar, what he detested about it the most was living in a fishbowl. He wanted to live his life by his own rules, but that was out the window when you reached his level of success.

Everyone was making money off of him so they were all invested in just about every aspect of his life. It was damn near impossible for Ian to convince what he called his money making team machine to go ahead and green light his divorce to Angela. They begged him to stay married in name only if possible, but Ian wasn't having it. He said he was too young to play those types of games for his public image. Although he didn't give a fuck either way, his team finally told him the move was acceptable since Angela was ecstatic to take a few million given she was entitled to nothing but child support due to the paltry pre-nup she signed, and to keep her mouth shut and not bash Ian in the media or disclose any terms of their divorce.

Ian was only a couple of weeks away from finalizing the divorce and being a bachelor again. He was looking forward to relishing in his freedom and enjoying life. That's why he questioned his decision to keep things going with Chantal. He knew exactly what type of woman she was and it had headache written all over it. He couldn't help but wonder if the real reason he wanted to keep Chantal around was because of her connection to Tyler. 'Til this day, Ian felt shortchanged that he and Tyler never had any real closure to their relationship. To know that she was now engaged to Chantal's ex made him curious. Ian had to know what about Andre Jackson Tyler found so irresistible that she was willing to risk her life to save his.

Chantal started jumping up and down with excitement when she hung up the phone with Ian. "I can't believe he called me!" she shrieked to an overwhelmed Shari.

"Ms. Thing, did that motherfucker lace you with something? Because you are bugging out over this dude. Damn, is the dick that official?"

"All jokes to the left, I don't know what it is. Something about him just got me open. The sex is ridiculous but it's more than that. He's just different than other dudes I've fucked with."

"Different how?" Shari couldn't help but start probing giving how stoked Chantal was over this guy.

"It's hard to explain, but most men I dealt with, including Andre, in the beginning, like Trina say, they *blah, blah, blah* you a lot. They might be open off some new pussy for a minute so they telling you whatever, but you sorta know they ain't really checking for you like that, although they try to make you think that they are. But a cat like Ian doesn't strike me as if he's playing those types of games. He might keep you around, but he basically lets you know his feelings aren't too deep about it. But then if he really does start checking for you on some serious shit, I believe he lets you know and he goes all out."

"Wow, that's interesting. So where do you stand right now with him?"

"I'm not quite sure. I think he's attracted to me physically but I don't think that's what motivated him to call me. It's something a little deeper than that but I haven't figured it out yet."

"Well when you find out please let me know."

"I got you, Thelma."

When Tyler woke up in the morning she didn't want to pull herself away from Andre's embrace. Having his muscular arms around her waist made her feel out of harm's way. She wished she could bottle this moment and carry it around with her all day, so every time she felt scared or alone she could remember how perfect her life was at this very minute. She eyed the clock and realized if she didn't get up now she would be late for work. She knew how William detested tardiness. So though every part of her body wanted to stay snuggled under Andre, she quietly glided from under him and went to the bathroom to take a shower.

After Tyler rushed to get dressed she kissed a still sleeping Andre on the lips and went downstairs. To her shock, her mother was sitting on the living room couch. "Mother, what are you doing here? I thought you went back to Atlanta."

"Good morning to you too, my dear."

"I didn't mean it like that. I'm just a little shocked to see you."

"I did go back to Atlanta but now I'm here again."

"Why?"

"I was worried about my daughter. I still see you and your sister as my little girls."

"Speaking of Ella, I'm going to see her when I go to New York in a few weeks. I miss her so much."

"She misses you too. She wanted to come when she heard about the accident, but you know during that time Fashion Week was approaching and she was swamped preparing for the show. I recently saw some of her designs and I must say I was very impressed."

"She has definitely stepped her game up. I'm so proud of her, my big sister a budding fashion designer. When I go to New York she has to hook me up."

"When are you leaving again?"

"In a few weeks. I wish it was tomorrow so I could be with Christian. He'll be with me during filming so I can spend time with him. After this movie is done I'm going to take an extended break so I can prepare for Christian to move to LA and live with me and Andre, especially since we're going to have a baby together." Tyler caught her mother rolling her eyes. "What's that about? I thought you said you'd accepted my relationship with Andre."

"I do, but I don't think you need to rush and start a family with him. You're on the path to be a huge star. Do you want to put that on hold so you can walk around with your belly poked out for nine months?"

"I don't know why I have these conversations with you, because you just don't get it. I love Andre and I want us to be a family. Having his baby would mean so much to me."

"Tyler, I know when I'm fighting a losing battle. Let's agree to disagree. Whatever decision you make, I'll support."

Tyler didn't quite believe her mother was being sincere but wanted the conversation to end all the same.

"So my dear, where are you off to this morning?"

"Work," Tyler answered as she walked to the kitchen to make her morning power shake.

"Work, so soon?"

"Yes, I started a new movie. I'm actually very excited about it."

"How nice. Why don't you let your mother accompany you to the set this morning? I would love to see my daughter in action."

"It's not that exciting, really."

"Let me be the judge of that."

"Maybe another time. It's been a little hectic these first few days."

"Tyler Blake, are you ashamed of having your mother on set with you?" Maria folded her arms and tapped her foot waiting for her daughter's response.

"Of course not. Fine, you can come." Tyler noticed her mother slightly smiling, no doubt feeling pleased with herself since she always got her way. *Some things never change,* Tyler thought to herself.

When Tyler and her mother arrived, the set was already abuzz. "Wow, this is awfully exciting!" Maria beamed, becoming instantly caught up in the aura of Hollywood.

"Yeah, I remember my first time on a movie set. It was the ultimate high," Tyler said, reflecting back to that time.

As the ladies walked in the direction of Tyler's trailer William noticed the pair. "Tyler, you look wonderful this morning," William said, greeting the women.

"I feel great."

"I'm happy to hear especially after that unfortunate incident."

"What incident?" Maria inquired.

"Mother, I'll tell you about it later."

"Mother, you're Tyler's mother? I knew I saw a resemblance but I assumed you were her sister. You look much too young to be her mother."

"Stop, you're making me blush."

"Yes, Mother, this is William, the director of the movie."

Maria's eyes widened. "It is a pleasure to meet you, William."

"The pleasure is mine. I won't keep you ladies as Tyler needs to get to hair and makeup. I'll see you shortly." William gave Tyler a kiss on the cheek and walked off, leaving Maria with a lustful glare in her eyes.

"That William is quite a handsome man."

"Yes he is and very intelligent. I have a great deal of respect for him."

"I would definitely like to get to know him better."

"Mother, I used to date William for a very long time before I fell in love with Andre."

Maria's mouth dropped. "What? He's old enough to be your father. You can't be serious?" Maria asked as they made their way to the trailer.

"I'm dead serious. At one time I thought we were very much in love, but I realized I was wrong. It was more of a misplaced father figure mentor love."

"My goodness, Tyler. You really *do* have daddy issues," Maria hissed as she sat down on the couch in the trailer.

"You sound like my best friend, Chrissie. But you're both right. I do have daddy issues, but what would you expect, especially since you ripped him out of my life when I was five years old." By the stunned look on her mother's face, Tyler knew she wasn't expecting for her to revisit such painful memories.

"Tyler, must we have this discussion again? It's not my fault your father never came back for you and your sister."

"If that was the truth, you would be right."

"Are you accusing me of lying about your father?"

"All I'm saying is that what I remembered of my dad, he would've never turned his back on us."

"You were a child, Tyler. You've created some fantasy world about your dad that is non existent. I know it must hurt, but unfortunately your father did turn his back on you. You have to accept that and let it go."

Before Tyler could respond they were interrupted by a knock at the door. "Who is it?"

"Ms. Blake, its T-Roc," the security guard answered.

Tyler opened the door, somewhat relieved that she had an excuse to end her conversation with her mother. Although she did want to get to the truth regarding her biological father, Tyler realized her mother would go to her grave sticking to her story.

"Tyler, I hope I'm not interrupting anything," T-Roc said, noticing Maria.

"No come in. My mother and I were catching up on the past but we're done now."

"Your mother? Now I see where you get all your beauty from."

"Who is this charming young man?"

"T-Roc. I'm co-starring in the movie with your daughter."

"How nice. You look awfully familiar." Maria paused for a moment trying to determine where she had seen the fine looking man before. "I remember. Don't you have a commercial for your signature cologne?"

"As a matter of fact I do," T-Roc answered with a smile.

"I never forget a face, especially one as gorgeous as yours. It was wonderful meeting you. I'll leave you two alone while I check out the set."

"Do you want one of the security guards to escort you around?" Tyler asked.

"No, dear, I'll be fine—trust me." Maria picked up her purse and headed out on a mission no doubt.

"Your mother is a very intriguing woman."

"Yes she is. So what's up?"

"Oh nothing. I was checking up on you. Yesterday when we spoke you were down because of Andre."

"I'm much better now. We had a wonderful evening," Tyler said gushing.

"Glad to hear. I know you have to get into hair and makeup so I'll see on the set in a little while."

"Okay. Oh, and T-Roc," he stopped and turned back to look at Tyler before walking out the door. "Thanks for your concern. I appreciate it."

"No problem." As T-Roc left he was heated about the turn of events. He was hoping that Andre would neglect Tyler and leave her vulnerable so he could be the shoulder for her to cry on. But of course, Andre had to get his act together. T-Roc felt time was not on his side and would need to act sooner rather than later.

Chantal was ecstatic about going to see Ian. She took her time getting dressed, making sure she was extra sexy for him. After dabbling on some lip gloss Chantal headed out the door to her destination.

As she drove to Ian's penthouse, she heard her cell phone ringing. "Hello."

"Kitten, how are you?"

At first Chantal thought that whoever was on the other end with that operatic voice must've had the wrong number until flaming ass Rupert popped in her head. "Rupert, how are you?"

"Better, now that I have you on the phone. You should be getting my agent agreement in the mail today."

"Wonderful. I'm out right now, but when I get home I'll send it to my attorney and have him look over it."

"Great! The sooner I get it back the sooner I'll make you a star."

"I simply love that word 'star', especially when it pertains to me."

"Well, kitten, you're on your way. I must be running...the world is calling me, but I'll be in touch. Tootles."

The idea of being a star had Chantal's adrenaline pumping. She put her foot down on the gas pedal and zoomed down the highway with visions of her name in bright lights.

Andre was stepping out of the shower when he heard the phone and answered the call.

"Hi, Andre, this is Chrissie."

"Chrissie, Tyler isn't here. She's on the set."

"I know. I wanted to speak with you."

Andre found that odd since he and Chrissie had never been on friendly terms. "What can I do for you?"

"The Magic Johnson Foundation is having a charity benefit tomorrow night, a star studded affair. I know its last minute, but I received a call asking if you and Tyler would be one of the presenters."

"I don't know, Chrissie. It has still been such a media frenzy with all this Chantal mess, and I don't know if Tyler is ready to handle all that."

"I know. Honestly, I got the request for you all to present a while ago but I held off on accepting because I wasn't sure how things would be with Tyler. But she seems strong and I think this would be great image building for the two of you as a couple in Hollywood. Andre, you have to get used to this. Once you and Tyler get married this will be your life."

"I'll discuss it with Tyler tonight and we'll get back to you."

"So you know, Andre, I could've gone directly to Tyler on this but I know you're an important part of her life. And I want us to start building a friendship."

"I appreciate that, Chrissie. I will speak to Tyler about this event and if she wants to go I promise we will be in attendance. Thanks again." When Andre hung up with Chrissie he had mixed feelings about the conversation. He was pleased that Chrissie was beginning to accept and respect his relationship with Tyler, but he was also coming to grips with what a Hollywood marriage would mean. It would change his whole lifestyle. In the music industry people expected you to fuck up and didn't dig so deep into your personal life. But it was a whole other ball game in this business. The media didn't wait for the drama to come to you; they went looking for it.

Chantal spread her curvaceous body across the bed after finishing up a third round of mind blowing sex with Ian. "You're incredible, you know that?" Chantal purred breathlessly.

"You're pretty wonderful too," Ian said, lighting up a blunt that was on the nightstand next to the bed.

"Doesn't the league have strict rules about things like that?"

"If you listen to David Stern they do, but only an idiot fails a drug test. They tell you in advance right before the season starts when the drug test is. If you pass then they don't test you for the remainder of the season. Only the stupid fucks who failed the initial test are subject to random drug testing."

"So that's how that works."

"Pretty much," Ian said, taking a pull. He motioned, offering Chantal some, and of course she obliged. After some back and forth the weed was taking affect and the mellow high kicked in.

"So, Ian, what happened between you and Tyler?" Chantal asked the question so out of the blue that Ian had his guard down. He found himself answering the question without even giving it a second thought.

"Tyler and I were young and in love. I made a lot of mistakes and so did she."

"That's not telling me much. Why you guys break up?"

"I really don't want to delve in the past."

"Why, did she break your heart?" Chantal asked jokingly, not thinking she would get a serious answer from Ian. But the premium weed was acting as a truth serum for him.

"As a matter of fact she did."

Chantal was stunned and the news made her sit up and shake her head trying to brush off the buzz. Ian had her attention before, but now he had her undivided attention. When he passed the blunt back to her, this time she declined.

"Really and how did she manage to do that?" Chantal was astounded that dainty Tyler could break the heart of a womanizing lover boy like Ian.

"Hmm, every time I think about that bullshit I want to break some shit. I'm still not fucking with my cousin behind that bullshit."

"Okay, I'm lost. What does your cousin have to do with you and Tyler breaking up?"

"She started fucking around with him behind my back and ended up pregnant. She claims I was the father, but she didn't know that shit for sure. I swear I wanted to kill both of them. I had never been that pissed or hurt in all my life. That shit still fucks with me to this day."

"Your cousin? Why would Tyler fuck your cousin when she had you?"

"I don't know. Maybe because he was some big music mogul that promised to make all her dreams come true. I still hate that bastard."

"Who's your cousin?"

"T-Roc," Ian said with hatred seething through his teeth.

Chantal damn near fell out the bed when Ian dropped that bombshell. She knew that Tyler wasn't as sweet as she appeared, but never guessed that she had done something that trifling.

"I had no idea T-Roc was your cousin."

"Yeah, most people don't, and frankly I don't claim him."

"But he's blood. How can you let Tyler come between family?

Ian gave Chantal an eerie stare. "At that time Tyler was my family too. T-Roc knew I planned on marrying her. She was everything to me, and like the toxin that he is, he couldn't stand that I had something he wanted. He plotted and schemed to take Tyler from me, and when she chose me over him, his ego couldn't handle it. T-Roc is the reason Tyler and I aren't together now."

"So whatever happened to the baby?" Chantal was on edge hearing the lurid details of the love triangle. She repeated her question to Ian, who seemed overwhelmed by the question.

"If you ever tell anybody this and they ask me, I'll deny it," he said solemnly.

Chantal nodded her head eager to hear the confession Ian obviously wanted to keep buried.

"When I found out Tyler was pregnant, I called all my family and friends sharing the news. When I told T-Roc, that cold motherfucker said that the baby could be his because he had been sleeping with Tyler too. If I could've reached through that phone I would be in jail for murder right now. I prayed that he was just being a hating ass bastard, but when I confronted Tyler I could tell by the look in her eyes that it was true. Man, my mind went blank. Next thing I knew, I threw her down the stairs and she had a miscarriage.

Chantal's heart was beating so fast. This information was more than she bargained for. Besides thinking about Tyler, she couldn't help but think about all the juicy tales for her upcoming novel, although that particular part of the story might have to remain in the dark. "Wow! I knew Tyler was no good, but my goodness, she's heartless!"

"Don't judge her. She was vulnerable and T-Roc took advantage of that. He's the heartless one, not Tyler."

"What is it about this woman?" Chantal barked, tossing the silk comforter off her body as she stepped out of the bed. "Andre, T-Roc, and now you defend Tyler like she's some fragile porcelain doll, when in all actuality she's a trifling bitch."

91

"So you know my cousin?"

"Yes, and I also knew he had some secrets on Tyler, but of course he wouldn't share them. His only concern was winning her over. Why he would want that trash I have no clue."

"T-Roc is still after her. It doesn't surprise me. He always has to get everything he wants no matter what the cost. I hope he never gets her."

"That's highly unlikely since she's engaged to my ex."

"You mean Andre. I heard about that. There were so many times I wanted to reach out to Tyler but she had moved on, and so did I. But now I'm about to be divorced so maybe..." Ian's voice trailed off.

Chantal couldn't believe what she was hearing. "You couldn't possibly want that harlot back!" Chantal screamed, revealing her jealousy.

"I didn't say that. But it doesn't matter, she's moved on to the next man."

"Please explain to me what you see in her. She cheated on you with your cousin and might've been carrying his baby. Why do you hate *him* and not *her*?

"Tyler may appear to have this ideal life, but she's been through hell, starting from childhood. She's made mistakes but she's got a lot of heart."

"Can someone gag me with a spoon, because I need to vomit. It's like my father always told me, 'Everybody has a sad story'. Tyler's life of hardship is no different than any other woman's, and she shouldn't get special treatment."

"It's understandable you would be bitter since Tyler ended up with your ex, but the hating is thick right now."

"The same way you believe T-Roc ruined your relationship with Tyler, she did the same to mine. I can't stand that self-righteous bitch and I'll be happy when somebody knocks her off that soapbox she's on!" Chantal secretly prayed it would be her.

Chapter Nine

Showdown

"I can't believe Chrissie talked you into going to this charity event tonight. She must have been awfully persuasive," Tyler teased as she slipped on her red Valentino gown.

"She does have a way with words, and damn you have a way of filling out a dress. Maybe we need to stay in tonight," Andre remarked after catching an eyeful of Tyler in the form fitting number.

"You're so silly. We'll have plenty of time for that when we get home. Now zip me up, please. Andre sprinkled kisses down Tyler's neck as he zipped up her dress. She closed her eyes about to melt from his touch. "Baby, if you don't stop we'll never make it out the front door."

"That's my intention."

"But you promised Chrissie, remember? We can't let the charity down."

Andre let out a deep sigh. "You're right, let's get out of here."

By the time Andre and Tyler arrived at the Beverly Hills Hilton the event was in full swing. The couple was swarmed by the paparazzi as they quickly walked down the red carpet. Tyler gave a brief wave and hello to a few familiar faces from media outlets, but followed Andre's lead as they held hands going inside, escaping the madness.

"Tyler, Andre over here," Chrissie said, waving at the pair.

When they walked up Chrissie introduced them to the lady who was overseeing the event. From the pleasant but shocked look on the woman's face it was clear she wasn't sure the two were going to show.

"Follow me. I'll show you to your table," Chrissie said, escorting them to where they'd be sitting. "But of course it's important the two of you mingle. Everyone is excited about meeting the both of you."

After Chrissie showed them their table Andre and Tyler decided to go outside to the pool area. Everything was decorated in complete white, from the lilies to the candles and the piano that John Legend was playing.

"It's beautiful out here. Let's dance, baby," Tyler said.

Andre took Tyler's hand and they began slow dancing by the edge of the pool to the melodic sounds coming from the piano as if no one else existed but them. Tyler held on tightly to Andre, relishing this magical moment. Life seemed perfect—almost too perfect.

"If it isn't the black Ken and Barbie of Hollywood."

Andre was the first to recognize the annoying voice and turned in her direction. "Chantal, what are you doing here?"

"And what are you doing with my dress on?" Tyler asked.

"I see we have more than just the same taste in men," Chantal countered.

Tyler was astonished that not only was Chantal at the same event with her, but had on the exact same dress, color and all.

"Who in the hell let you in anyway?" Andre asked, about to drag Chantal out with his bare hands.

"I was invited."

"By who?" Andre demanded to know.

"There you are. I was wondering where you disappeared to," Ian said, walking towards the threesome with two champagne glasses in his hands. With Andre blocking a clear view of Tyler, he didn't see her until he approached Chantal. They both stared at one another, unable to speak a word.

"Cat has your tongue, Tyler? You know Ian very well. Say hello." Chantal couldn't disguise the gloating in her voice.

"Tyler, how are you?" Ian asked in a low tone, looking at her as if he was seeing a ghost.

"I'm fine. Is Chantal your guest? Because if so, can you please escort her out of here?"

"If you have something to say, Tyler, you direct it to me."

"Chantal, I try not to have conversations with deranged, jilted brides who try to run people over in their wedding gowns. Ian, this is the type of company you're keeping now?"

"Tyler, it isn't like that," Ian said, walking towards Tyler, but Andre's reflexes kicked in and he moved his body forward so Ian couldn't get near her.

Chantal used the opening to get in Tyler's face. "You think you're so much better than me. But I know all your dirty little secrets. You're nothing but a slut!" Chantal shouted, pointing her finger in Tyler's face. Andre and Ian were so busy exchanging words they weren't paying attention to the altercation brewing between the women.

"Slut? That's the best you can do? You're so pathetic, Chantal. I almost pity you. Now move out my way before I call security and have them toss you away like the trash you are."

"How dare you!" Chantal roared as she grabbed Tyler's arm.
"Let me go!"

"You're not going anywhere until Andre hears what type of woman you really are." Tyler yanked her arm from Chantal's grip. "Andre, your precious Tyler is nothing but a slut."

"Chantal, shut up!" both Ian and Andre said simultaneously.

"Not until I'm finished saying what I have to say. Andre, you're always so quick to tear me down. But your sweet little Tyler isn't sweet at all. Tyler's past is quite checkered. Not only was she having sex with Ian, but she was fucking his cousin, T-Roc at the same time. And she was so careless with her sex-escapades that she became pregnant and didn't know who the father was. That's the real Tyler. Not the one who you have on a pedestal."

Tyler grabbed a drink from a passing waiter and tossed it in Chantal's face. "You conniving bitch!"

"Yuk, you've ruined my makeup and my dress!" The rage instantly hit Chantal and she raised her hand back and slapped the shit out of Tyler. Tyler didn't hold back and smacked her right back, but instead of a flat hand, with a balled fist. "You punched me!"

By the time Andre snapped out of his daze and tried to break up the quarrel, the women were now in a full-fledged brawl that had them grabbing onto each other's hair, tripping in their heels and falling into the pool splashing water on the entire viewing audience.

"What is going on?" Chrissie asked Andre as she came up to see what all the commotion was about. They were all standing at the edge of the pool with their hands outstretched trying to pull the ladies out the water, but their fighting continued oblivious to eyes being on them. "Tell me that isn't Tyler in that pool. Oh my goodness, this is a total nightmare. Who is that in the water with her?"

"Chantal," Andre stated, only half-way paying attention to Chrissie.

"Security, get that woman out of the water and out of this event! There is a restraining order against her and she isn't supposed to come within a hundred feet of Tyler. Get her out of here now! How in the hell did she even get in this party?" Chrissie trilled.

"Chantal came as Ian Addison's date," Andre informed her.

"Ian, you're responsible for bringing this poison to this event?"

"Chrissie, I had no idea Tyler was going to be here. I apologize."

"I see you're still the same immature prick you've always been. I want you out of here, and take your floozy with you."

Tyler and Chantal were now both out of the pool, drenching wet. Andre took off his jacket and put it around Tyler's shoulder. "Are you okay?"

"I'm fine."

"Tyler, I'm so sorry. If I knew you were going to be here I would've never brought Chantal."

"How could you talk to her about something so private that happened between the two of us?"

Ian put his head down in shame.

"Wait, what Chantal said is really true?"

"Damn right, it's true, Andre. That hussy ain't shit!" Chantal spit.

"Officers, this is the lady you need to arrest right here," Chrissie said pointing to Chantal.

"Arrest! For what?" Chantal demanded to know.

"You're violating the restraining order against you."

"Is that true, miss?" one of the officers questioned.

"She hit me first!"

"I'll take that as a 'yes'. Miss, put your hands behind your back."

As the officer handcuffed Chantal she became belligerent calling them every name in the book. "Andre, do something! You can't let them arrest me. This is all Tyler's fault. Don't you see what type of woman she is?" Chantal continued her chastising as she was hauled out of the function. All you saw were intense stares and loud whispers from the crowd.

"Tyler, you need to get out of here. I'll have you leave out the back so you can avoid the paparazzi," Chrissie insisted.

Tyler and Andre both followed Chrissie out. They were all relieved when there wasn't a camera in sight. They got in the awaiting car and Tyler lay back in the seat mortified by what happened. There was complete silence for the duration of the ride home.

Before Tyler even made it to the bedroom she had ripped off her twenty-five thousand dollar Valentino dress, leaving it at the edge of the stairs. Andre followed behind her, desperate for answers to the millions of questions occupying his mind. By the time he reached the bedroom Tyler was already in the shower and the bathroom door was locked. He wanted to kick it down but knew that wouldn't solve anything, so he waited patiently on the bed trying to calm down. He finally felt he had control over his anger until the door unlocked and he was face to face with Tyler.

"What the hell was Chantal talking about back there at the party? And don't pretend you don't know what I'm talking about because I heard what you said to Ian, and that was damn near an admission of guilt."

Tyler didn't say a word as she walked past Andre towards the closet. Andre was stunned that Tyler was ignoring him. He stood in the closet entrance watching her flip through the plush satin hangers deciding which nightgown would grace her body before going to bed. After deciding on the silver silk baby doll with pearl and sequin embellishments, an empire waist, plunging neckline and side slits—the sort of get-up that would have any man with a pulse forget his misery—Tyler dropped her towel and slipped it on. She slowly brushed past Andre, and he hoped she didn't feel his erection when doing so.

Andre refused to give in to his lustful desire. As much as he wanted to take off his clothes, crawl into bed and make love to Tyler, he decided to use his upper head instead of his lower. "Tyler, are you going to answer my question?" he asked, still keeping his distance. He feared that if he went any closer and inhaled her intoxicating scent he wouldn't be able to control himself.

"What question?" Tyler asked as if she had no clue what he was talking about, which infuriated him.

"Don't play games with me, Tyler. I'd expect that from Chantal but not from you."

"Oh, so now you're comparing me to that psycho?"

Andre put his hands over his face trying to understand how Tyler was flipping this around like he was in the wrong. "No, I'm not. Let me start over with this: What was your relationship with Ian and T-Roc? What happened?"

"Honestly, I don't think it's any of your business. It's the past and it should be left there. You don't hear me asking you about every woman you were in a relationship with, although it seems you still can't get rid of one of them."

"Listen, T-Roc isn't in the past. You're filming a movie with him right now in the present. If you were involved with him, it would explain why he is so determined to stay in your life. We shouldn't keep secrets from each other, Tyler. All it will do is cause us not to trust one another."

"So you have no secrets about your relationships that you rather keep in the past and not share with me?"

"No, I don't. That is why I want you to tell me about your relationship with Ian and T-Roc, because we shouldn't keep secrets from each other."

"Fine. Years ago when I first got to New York I dated T-Roc briefly. It didn't work. Then I met Ian. I had no idea they were cousins. By the time I found out, I was already in love with Ian. Then we had a huge falling out, one that T-Roc orchestrated so I could run into his arms, which I did. I soon realized that I still loved Ian and that T-Roc was the one behind all the drama, so Ian and I got back together."

"A few weeks later I found out I was pregnant and I didn't know who the father was. But it didn't matter because when Ian shared the news with his family, T-Roc was more than happy to announce that the baby could be his. Of course Ian lost it and he threw me down the stairs, which made me have a miscarriage."

"Are you satisfied now hearing my dirty little secret? If you like, I can share all of them with you as I have so many."

Andre stood in the center of the bedroom speechless. He knew Tyler's confession wouldn't be anything nice, but he wasn't expecting her to admit to such foul behavior. "I can't believe I'm hearing this. How could you do something like that?"

"That is exactly why I didn't want to tell you, because I would have to endure that look of disgust and disappointment on your face. Don't you think I feel ashamed by my actions? You'll never understand the pain I went through knowing that because of what I did, the baby I was carrying died. I don't need for you to pass judgment against me."

"But you made yourself seem so perfect, as if you could do no wrong."

"What woman are you describing right now? When I met you I was involved with a married man. I have never presented myself as some martyr. I'm probably one of the most flawed individuals you'll ever meet. But I do have a conscience, and everyday I'm working towards healing myself so I can be a better person. It's a process though, and not something that will happen overnight. For you to stand there and make me feel less than human isn't helping."

"I want to understand, but it's hard."

"I was nineteen. You never did stupid things as a teenager that you wish you could take back?"

"Okay, so you were young. But how can you still work with T-Roc?"

"Because this is business and I have a professional obligation. Of course working with T-Roc isn't my first choice, but at the same time this is William's movie and I'm an actress. I have a job to do. That's like saying I can't do another movie that William is directing because I slept with him."

"If I had my way you wouldn't be working with either one of them. There is going to come a point when you'll have to decide what is more important to you."

"Andre, you know I want us to be a family. Me, you, Christian, Melanie and the babies I want us to have together. But I also want to fulfill my dream of being a superstar. Is that so terrible?"

"But at what price? Doing love scenes with a man I despise? Being directed in a movie by a man that I despise? And let's not forget you've slept with both of them. Only in Hollywood would this bullshit be acceptable." Andre grabbed his car keys from the dresser and headed towards the door.

"Andre, where are you going?"

"I have to get out of here and clear my mind."

"Please don't leave. I want to fall asleep in your arms."

"Not tonight," he said before storming out.

Chapter Ten

The Thrill is Gone

Chantal sat on the cold steel bench wondering how in the hell she ended up back in jail. She hadn't slept a wink and felt that the walls were closing in on her. Her eyes scanned the small holding cell that occupied five sleeping females, all of whom looked liked broken down prostitutes. Upon her arrival last night, Chantal placed her one phone call to her attorney, begging him to get her out. It was late and Chantal assumed he hadn't yet got her message, but that didn't keep her from calling everyone in the building a four letter word as if it was their fault she violated her restraining order.

"Chantal Morgan," the guard called out.

All the ladies miraculously woke up from their snoozing and raised their hands, "That's me."

"I'm Chantal Morgan," she said rolling her eyes and smacking her lips.

"Who the hell do she think she is?" Chantal heard one of the other inmates say.

"She probably a call girl, but that don't make her no better than the rest of us. We just walk the streets in search of our clients and they find her snobby ass in the Yellow Pages."

"I ain't no call girl, thank you very much," Chantal barked.

"Then you just a dummy for ending up in here," another female shot back, and all the ladies burst out laughing.

"Everybody quiet," the guard yelled. Chantal slit her eyes at the women before heading out. "Your attorney is here to see you."

Praise the Lord! Chantal thought to herself. She practically leaped across the hall trying to get to her attorney. "Mitchell, I'm so happy to see you," Chantal said as she sat down for the face-to-face.

"Chantal, we really have to stop meeting under these circumstances."

Chantal could tell by the frown on Mitchell's face that he wasn't pleased, and she couldn't blame him. "I know, but it wasn't my fault. That prima donna, Tyler threw champagne in my face and on my dress. I had no choice but to retaliate."

"Have you already forgotten there is a restraining order in place? You should've never been close enough to get in Ms. Blake's face."

"Oh please, what was I supposed to do, leave the event because the queen of the night decided to grace us with her presence? I was there first. *She* should've left."

"Chantal," Mitchell said firmly, and by his tone Chantal knew he was growing impatient with her. "The restraining order isn't against Tyler, it's against you. That's why you're in jail and she's not."

"Fine. I understand I got myself in a pickle of a situation, but I need to get out of here."

"I don't know if it's gong to be that easy. It hasn't even been a month and you've already violated the terms of your plea agreement. A judge may decide to throw the book at you and keep you locked up for the duration of your probation."

"Wait, wait, wait a minute. My probation is for years."

"Yes, I know…ten to be exact."

"I can't stay in jail for ten years. I can't stay in this hell hole for another day. Please, Mitchell, you have to get me out of here!"

"I'll do the best I can. I have a hearing scheduled this afternoon. Hopefully I'll get a judge that I play golf with and he'll be lenient. But Chantal, this is it. I don't know how much longer the person who is footing your bill is going to keep this up. And I promise you, my services are far from cheap," Mitchell reminded Chantal as he grabbed his briefcase and stood up ready to leave.

"I promise I'll get my act together, but don't worry about the money. Pretty soon I'll be able to afford you on my own. Didn't you get the contract from the agent? He's going to get me a seven figure book deal. And that doesn't include speaking engagements or other things I'll get paid for," Chantal said, grinning about her future prospects as a literary star.

Mitchell sat back down and stared at Chantal. "Yes, I did read over the contract and I'm very familiar with Rupert Douglass."

"Then you know I'm about to be in the money," Chantal said, singing her own praises.

"I'm assuming this is a tell-all."

"No doubt, and with the episode that happened last night and the juicy news I found out about little miss, perfect Tyler Blake, I'm sure Rupert will up that book deal to the high seven figures as I have a lot to reveal."

"That book will never make it into publication."

"What are you talking about?"

"Did you not read over the plea agreement you signed? Better yet, were you listening when I read it to you?"

"Of course I was, but what does that have to do with my salacious book?"

Mitchell let out an annoyed sigh. "Chantal, part of the plea agreement with you getting no jail time was that you can't profit because of what happened to the victims, which is Andre and Tyler."

"I don't understand. They're not victims."

"In the eyes of the law they are. You tried to run them over, remember?"

"So what? I can't include in my book the torment Andre caused me by leaving me at the altar on my wedding day so he could run off with Tyler, which pushed me over the edge and caused me to run them over in the first place?"

"Legally you can tell the story as long as neither Tyler nor Andre is ever mentioned, or is it even insinuated that the characters are based on their likeness. But then, what publisher would care about your story if you can't mention the stars?"

"How in the hell did you allow me to sign an agreement like that? You're my lawyer; you're supposed to protect my best interests."

"I did, and that was making sure you didn't spend the rest of your life behind bars, although at the pace you're going it's becoming increasingly impossible." Chantal put her head down, on the verge of tears. "Chantal, I had no idea that being an author was so important to you," Mitchell said sarcastically.

"It's not. But bringing down Tyler Blake is. Telling this story would allow the world to see her for the home wrecker she is. Now you're telling me I can't even do that."

"I really must be going because I have to call in some favors in an attempt to get you released from jail... hopefully today. But before I go, I have to give you some much needed advice. Get over your obsession with Ms. Blake. It will cause you nothing but grief and possibly your life. No one is worth that, not even a Hollywood star."

Chantal sulked in her chair as she watched Mitchell Stern leave. She knew he was right, but it was as if Tyler had infected her mind and body. There seemed to be no cure to rid Tyler from Chantal's system. But as the guard escorted Chantal back to the holding cell, she decided she would have to find a way to get over it unless she wanted to spend the rest of her life locked up.

When Tyler arrived on set the first thing she did was go searching for William. She needed someone to talk to, and even though William didn't care for Andre, he would at least listen to her vent and Tyler could trust that he wouldn't share their conversation with anyone else. "Hi, have you seen William?" Tyler asked one of the production assistants.

"Did you check his office?"

"Yeah, but he wasn't in there."

"I saw him headed towards the room in the back about twenty minutes ago," another assistant said, pointing her in the right direction.

"Thanks." Tyler was anxious to get to William. After their blow up, Andre didn't come back home and Tyler was devastated. She hoped that William could calm her nerves, but he did just the opposite.

"What in the hell is wrong with you two?" Tyler yelled when she opened the door and found her mother spread across the table and kissing William passionately as his body thrust inside of her.

The piercing of Tyler's voice snapped them out of their sex session and both turned their faces catching a glimpse of the repulsion in her eyes. "Tyler, it isn't what you think," William sputtered weakly.

Both Tyler and her mother glared at William like he was crazy.

"I think I know what fucking looks like, William. But you and my mother! I don't know which one of you disgusts me more."

"Dear, we can explain," Maria said coolly. She seemed to be the only one unaffected by what was transpiring.

"Save it. I so can't deal with this right now. But I advise that next time you want to go at it like dogs in heat, lock the door."

William pulled himself from Maria, pissed that Tyler had caught them in the compromising position.

"What are you doing? We're not done yet," Maria exclaimed.

"You're daughter caught us having sex. Yes, we are done."

"Please, William. Tyler will be fine."

"I have to go explain."

"Explain what? That two consenting adults gave into their mutual attraction and had sex?"

"I'll let her know it was an accident."

"Oh, so you're going to tell Tyler that all six times we had sex was an accident?"

"I knew this was wrong. With everything that Tyler has been going through she doesn't need another disappointment."

"Tyler is much stronger than everyone gives her credit for. She'll get over it. As a matter of fact, she's probably already forgotten. Trust me, she's my daughter and I know her better than anybody."

T-Roc noticed Tyler walking towards her trailer and she was visibly upset. "Tyler, what's wrong?" he asked, pulling her over to the side so they could have some privacy.

"This isn't a good time. I really want to go to my trailer and be alone."

"You're too upset. I don't think it's a good idea for you to be alone." T-Roc lifted Tyler's chin so he could stare her directly in the eyes. "I told you that if you ever needed to talk I would be here for you." Without warning Tyler broke down and started crying and T-Roc held her in his arms. "Tyler, it'll be okay," T-Roc said reassuringly.

"No it's not. Everything is going so wrong. Andre is furious at me and I feel like I'm losing him."

"Why, what happened?" T-Roc's voice sounded genuinely concerned so Tyler began purging her soul.

"Andre found out about the past we shared."

"How did that happen?"

"From Chantal."

"Who told Chantal?" T-Roc knew for a fact that he never divulged the history that he shared with Tyler, although Chantal inquired on more than one occasion. He couldn't begin to imagine who could've told her since all parties involved were very private."

"Your cousin, Ian."

"What! Are you sure?"

"Positive. I ran into both of them last night at this charity event. Chantal was Ian's date. I guess she's sleeping with him now. The devious bitch totally blew up my spot last night right in front of Andre. When we got home I confirmed her story. I mean there was no sense in lying. But Andre was furious with me. He stormed out and didn't come home last night."

"Tyler, calm down. Andre is just blowing off some steam. He'll realize that we all have secrets that we want to keep in the dark and you're no exception. Andre will forgive you."

"I don't think so. I tried to get him to understand exactly what you just said, but Andre is adamant that he doesn't have any secrets that he's keeping from me and I'm the only one with the shameful past. I feel like such a loser right now. It's like no matter how hard you try there is no escaping your past. I don't understand why Andre can't take me as I am."

"I know you probably don't want to hear this, but I love you just the way you are, Tyler, never stopped. No woman that I've ever met compares to you. I know that I made multiple mistakes in our relationship, and I hope that one day you'll forgive me. I've accepted that you've moved on with Andre and I truly want you to be happy. Although I've always believed that we belong together, I won't cross the line because I know you're committed to Andre. But believe me, Andre knows how special you are and he will come around. It will all work out for the best, trust me."

"Thank you so much, T-Roc. More and more I'm realizing that you have changed. In the past you would've used this opportunity to manipulate me and the situation, but instead you're giving me encouragement as a friend. You don't know how much that means to me."

"Yes, I do, and I mean every word. You know Andre isn't one of my favorite people, but he loves you. It's hard for a man like him who is open about his past and doesn't keep secrets to then find out that the woman he loves has been."

"Wow, never did I think I would hear you defending Andre."

"Me neither, but like you've said, I've changed. I'm trying to look at this situation from a non-selfish point of view."

"I appreciate that. I'm glad that you stopped me and we talked. I feel so much better. Thank you."

Chrissie watched discretely as T-Roc walked Tyler to her trailer and she was livid. She had been eavesdropping for the majority of their conversation and couldn't believe how thick the bullshit T-Roc was laying on was. The worst part was that Tyler was falling for it. But she couldn't blame her because T-Roc had fooled her too. But the jig was up because Chrissie planned on having a heart-to-heart with Tyler and revealing all.

After filming ended for the day T-Roc was anxious to reach his destination. It was time for his informant to drop the ball on Andre Jackson once and for all. Tyler was becoming more vulnerable and it was the perfect opportunity to bring an end to their relationship. Andre was the fool to judge Tyler so harshly, especially with the skeleton in his closet. Once Tyler realized that her checkered past is a misdemeanor compared to Andre's, then she'll be through with him for good, and T-Roc would be right there picking up the pieces.

T-Roc pulled up to the back of the warehouse that was located on the outskirts of LA. His informant was expecting him, and since they rarely met in person, he knew it must be serious.

"What's up man?" the informant asked as he opened the door to let T-Roc in.

"It's all good, Gee." They shook each other's hands as Gee closed the door behind T-Roc. "You know, as long as we've been doing business together you've never told me what 'Gee' is short for."

"The same reason I never asked you how you came up with the name T-Roc. It's just a name, my man."

"I feel you. Well as long as you keep delivering on the goods like you always do, I'll call you whatever you like." They both let out a playful chuckle and then got down to business. "It's time for you to leak that information about Andre Jackson to your reporter friend. I want that shit splashed across the front page of Friday's paper."

"That won't be a problem as long as you got what I need."

T-Roc reached in his coat pocket and pulled out the envelope containing the twenty-five thousand dollars. "You'll get the other half once the story hits," T-Roc said, handing Gee the money.

"Then I'll be seeing you Friday so I can collect."

"No doubt." When T-Roc got up to leave he couldn't help but notice that underneath the perfectly tailored white pinstriped button-down classic fit shirt with spread collar and round hem, complimented by well-crafted double pleated black pants and Gucci leather loafers, if you looked closer, Gee had the most sinister eyes. But T-Roc didn't care because he always got the job done.

"**Tyler, we need to talk,**" **Chrissie** said as Tyler was gathering her stuff about to leave for the day.

"If it's about last night's charity event, I'm sorry. I feel so embarrassed. I can't believe it wasn't in today's paper."

"Luckily the photographers there were in-house and they all signed agreements that prohibited them to print any photos that weren't approved first. I also placed a few calls to my tabloid connections and they promised to keep a lid on it. I'm sure there'll be at least one rookie eager to leak the story, and of course Perezhilton.com, but nothing we can't sweep under the rug."

"Once again, you're the best. I just wish Andre would take the high road and sweep this mess under the rug."

"It's not your fault that his crazy baby mama can't control herself. She had no business being there in the first place."

"I agree, but it wasn't the fight that he's furious about, it's what led up to the fight."

"I don't understand."

"During pillow talk I suppose Ian told Chantal about the scandalous past we share, and of course she couldn't wait to tell Andre all about it at the event."

"I missed all of that. That woman is lethal."

"Who are you telling? I can't believe Andre was ever involved with someone so treacherous, and then had a baby with her. But then again we all make mistakes, I should know."

"Don't be so hard on yourself. I mean Andre is definitely no saint. What happened with Ian is in the past."

"True, but the T-Roc aspect of it is what bothers him more than anything. I guess I can't blame him. But I tried to explain that T-Roc and I have a working relationship, and because we slept with each other in the past don't mean a thing. Of course Andre wasn't trying to hear that. But you know, I think Andre is being too hard on T-Roc. I think he's really changed."

"Speaking of T-Roc, that's..."

Before Chrissie could drop the bomb on T-Roc about all his scheming, Maria barged in.

"Mother, I'm not in the mood to speak to you right now.

"Hello, Chrissie."

"Hi, Maria, how are you?"

"Great, can't you tell?" Maria said as she did a side turn showing off her still perfect size six figure. Chrissie grinned because there was no denying that Maria was a stunning looking woman for her age, or any other for that matter. "Chrissie, dear, I really need to speak with my daughter. Can you excuse us?"

"Mother, we were in the middle of a very important conversation so why don't you leave?"

"Tyler, its okay. What I have to say can wait. Talk to your mother. As always, it was nice seeing you again."

Maria waited until Chrissie walked out and the door was shut before speaking.

"Whatever you have to say, I don't want to hear it."

"Is that any way to speak to your mother?"

"Well, when I get a mother I'll ask her."

"Tyler, how can you say such a thing?"

"How could you have sex with a man that I used to be in love with?"

"Let's be honest. You were never in love with William."

"So maybe I wasn't, but there was a time that I thought I was and I slept with him, for heaven's sake. How could you turn around and have sex with a man that your daughter was intimate with?"

"Dear, your relationship with William is in the past and it should be left there. It's not like you're still sleeping with him. You really need to be mature about this. William is destroyed that you're so upset with him."

"He should be. William was my mentor and the person I turned to for advice."

"And he still can be."

"Don't you get it? Every time I see him now I'll have flashbacks of the two of you having sex on a table."

"The visual could be worse. Both William and I are extremely sexy."

"Yuk! Goodbye, Mother. I'll talk to you later." Tyler grabbed her belongings and left her mother standing in the trailer alone.

Maria couldn't comprehend why her daughter was overreacting, but reasoned she would soon come to her senses and get over it.

Chapter Eleven

Killing Me Softly

Chantal had to sit in jail for three more days before her attorney was able to get her out. "Mitchell, I can't believe it took you three days to get me sprung from that despicable place. What happened to all your high powered connections?"

"You're out aren't you? So let's just leave it at that."

"Whatever. I just want to go home and take a shower. You are giving me a ride home, right?"

"Actually, that car parked right over there will be taking you home."

Chantal looked in the direction that Mitchell was pointing and the only car she saw was a black Bentley with dark tinted windows. "You're talking about that Bentley?"

"Yes."

"Who sent that car for me?"

"When you get in ask the driver. I really must be going. But if you want to get home I suggest you get in that car."

Chantal reluctantly walked towards the car trying to get a peek as to who was inside. If she wasn't so desperate for a bath and a hot meal she might've declined the waiting ride, but Chantal was in no position to turn down anything, especially since she had absolutely no money on her.

When she reached the car and opened the door, her mouth dropped. "T-Roc! What are you doing here?"

"I put up the money for your bail, so why not pick you up?"

"You paid for my bail, why?" Chantal questioned as she got in the car and shut the door.

"Think of me as your secret Santa, except I'm not a secret anymore."

Chantal knew that all this playing on words meant something, but she hadn't figured out what yet. Then like a bright light going off in her head it hit her. "You're the one who has been paying all of my legal expenses. You hired Mitchell Stern and paid the million-dollar bail. But why? I mean we did have great sex at one time, but did I make you feel the earth move to that point?"

T-Roc let out a boisterous laugh. "That's what I love about you, Chantal, your over-the-top sense of humor."

"That can't possibly be the only thing you love about me."

"Of course not."

"Seriously, T-Roc, you don't do anything without a reason. What gives?"

"You're no good to me locked up. If you're in jail how can you put a wedge between Tyler and Andre?"

"I doubt I'm having that affect on them. From what I've seen, they're happier than ever."

"How wrong you are. That little outburst you had at the charity event the other night has really put a damper on the lovebirds. Andre is having a hard time accepting that Tyler used to be involved with me."

"Oh good. That made my brief stint being locked up worthwhile."

"Then I guess that means you don't mind that I had you kept there for an extra three days."

"Excuse me?"

"Yes. Of course with all of Mitchell's connections he was able to get you released on Tuesday, but I thought you needed some time to clear your head and think."

"You're telling me I could've been out of that dump on Tuesday but you purposely kept me there? How dare you!"

"How soon we forget. If it wasn't for me you would be doing much longer than three days. You could never afford an attorney like Mitchell Stern, and Andre was in no rush to get you out of jail the first time around, and it didn't seem that my cousin Ian was too eager for this go round. I seem to be the only man you can count on, Chantal, so you should show more gratitude for my kindness."

"Who told you about me and your cousin? I know it wasn't Ian since you all don't speak any longer. It's amazing how Tyler wreaks havoc wherever she goes."

"No, Chantal, that would be your specialty. You seem to forget that you're no longer in Southside, Chicago. Engaging in public brawls just isn't the thing to do. But speaking of Tyler, I want you to leave her alone. For now on she is off limits."

"But I thought you just said that you liked me putting a rift between her and Andre."

"I do, and you can harass Andre as much as you like, just make sure Tyler isn't part of that harassment."

"You still think you have a chance with her, don't you?"

"Of course I do. I have a very strong feeling that soon Andre will need someone to nurse a broken heart. Maybe you can be that someone."

"What have you've done now?"

"I haven't done a thing."

"Can you please just tell me why?"

"Why what?"

"Why you're so determined to have Tyler to yourself. There are thousands of women out there. What makes her so special?"

"If I knew the answer to that then she wouldn't be special now would she? I would love to sit here and play these question games with you, but you're home."

Chantal looked out the window and saw she was in front of her condo complex. She was hoping to have a little more time to pick T-Roc's brain, but that wouldn't be the case. "I appreciate the ride home and everything else you've done for me. Bye for now, but I'm sure we will cross paths again."

"I'm positive we will too. But, Chantal, remember what I said; stay away from Tyler. You know how quickly my kindness can turn to vengeance." With that T-Roc slammed the door and the driver drove off barely giving Chantal a chance to step on the curb.

When Chantal reached her front door she was greeted by several piled up newspapers, and at the very top was the LA Times with the headline, *"Hollywood Royalty or Would Be Murderer?"* and underneath there was a mug shot of Andre Jackson.

Tyler dropped her power shake when she picked up the morning paper. The glass splattered on the kitchen floor spilling the drink over her crisp white sneakers and baby blue track suit.

"Ms. Blake, are you okay?" Deanna, the maid asked, startled by the loud crash from the glass.

"No I'm not. Can you please clean this mess up?"

"Of course, but what's wrong?"

"Everything! Did you see today's paper with this mug shot of Andre?" she asked, holding up the newspaper.

"No, I didn't."

"They're saying all sorts of terrible things about him, and I hope none of its true."

"You're so upset. Sit down and I'll make you something to eat."

"Thank you, but I have to go." Tyler ran out of the kitchen, gripping the newspaper. Before becoming hysterical she wanted to speak to Andre. He still hadn't come home in the last few days, instead staying in a bungalow at the Beverly Hills Hotel. Tyler had only spoken to him briefly a few times because he told her he needed time to think, but this couldn't wait.

With security guards in tow, Tyler had her driver take her to the hotel. As they were leaving, the paparazzi swarmed the car when the gate opened. Because the driver was skilled and used to the shenanigans, he had no problem maneuvering his way past them without his vehicle causing bodily harm.

Tyler's cell phone was blowing up like crazy but she ignored each call until Andre's number popped up.

"Andre, what is going on?"

"Where are you?"

"In the car on my way to see you."

"Okay, we'll talk when you get here."

Tyler was hoping that the first thing Andre would've of said when she answered the phone was that the article was nothing but a big fabricated lie, but he didn't. She was getting a nauseated feeling in the pit of her stomach and it was scaring her.

When they arrived at the hotel the driver pulled around to a back location that a lot of high profile celebrities used when they wanted to avoid the media or not be seen by the general public. Tyler had one of the security guards escort her to the bungalow, and he stayed posted outside in case there was any drama.

After Andre opened the door, he walked back over to the living room area and sat down on the couch not saying a word to Tyler. She could see the newspaper article on top of the table and went over to pick it up. "Are you going to explain this to me?"

"I'm sure you read it. It's pretty self-explanatory."

"Are you telling me what they're saying in this article is true?"

"What do you think?"

"I don't think you're a murderer. But I need to know what happened."

"I don't want to talk about it."

"You can't be shutting me out. You're the same man that hasn't been home all week because you're so pissed at me for not telling you about my past relationships with two men. Now you have the audacity to say you don't want to talk about it. What happened to that great speech about not having any secrets? That was all a lie?"

"This is different. Somebody is playing with my life. When I find out who the motherfucker is that leaked this story, I swear I'm going to rip their head off!" Andre said before ripping the plug out the wall as he picked up a lamp and threw it across the room.

"Ms. Blake, are you okay?" the security asked while banging on the door.

"I'm fine." Tyler paused and turned back to Andre. "You need to calm down."

"Don't tell me to calm down. Ever since I came to this bullshit town and got involved with you I've been in a twilight zone. These Hollywood phonies will do anything to get a story and use it to destroy your life. Hollywood royalty or would be murderer—what sort of garbage is this?" Andre said, tossing the paper on the floor.

"You blame me for all of this?"

"You're the one so desperate to be a movie star. If it wasn't for you I would've been left this place and went back to New York."

"No one forced you to audition for 'Angel'. That was your decision. So obviously you wanted to be a movie star just like me."

"Maybe at first, but I told you a long time ago that the stakes are way too high. These people will cross any boundaries to get what they want. And somebody is going through a lot of trouble to bring me down. These records are sealed. They were supposed to be buried so deep that not even the FBI would be able to recover them."

"Andre, are you going to tell me what happened?"

"What difference would it make? The media is going to put their spin on it anyway. They'll have fact and fiction so convoluted that *I* won't even know what really happened anymore."

"Baby, please don't shut me out," Tyler pleaded.

"I think we need to end this for a while. Take a break and see what happens."

"Andre, you can't mean that."

"I do. I need you to leave," he said coldly.

Tyler ran to him, latching onto his arm begging him to take it back. But he didn't. Instead, he pushed her away, went to the bedroom and locked the door. Tyler banged on the door crying her heart out for five minutes, but she realized Andre had turned the volume on the television all the way up to drown out her pleas. Tyler was crushed. She couldn't accept the fact that the love of her life had rejected her.

"Shari, did you hear about Andre?" Chantal asked, standing up and reading the article for the hundredth time. She was so engrossed that the long bath and hot meal she dreamed about having while in jail still eluded her.

"Damn sure have. But before we get to that, where in the hell have you been?"

"You haven't spoken to Jalen?"

"Nope, not since I got back to Chicago. He left a message for me yesterday, but when I called him back it went straight to voice mail. Why?"

"Girl, I've been locked up for the last few days."

"Bitch, stop lying!"

"Girl, I ain't lying. I went to this shindig with Ian and ran into Tyler and Andre. I had to check that bitch and that turned into a heated argument with blows being exchanged, and of course I ended up in jail."

"What, over a fight?"

"Can you believe that? I mean getting knocked around is how you handle your business where we from, but these corny ass motherfuckers ain't having that shit. Some silly ass white broad ran and told the cops that I was violating my restraining order so they arrested me."

"Damn! Where was Ian at during all this?"

"Over there kissing Tyler's ass, apologizing for bringing me. Can you believe that shit? Ian didn't even come to check for me, bail me out or nothing. I ain't feeling this town. These people on some other shit. Point proved, look what they doing to Andre."

"Oh yeah, back to that. We'll finish discussing your incident later 'cause I know they're some blank spots I need you to fill in."

"I got you. But yeah, they got my baby daddy all splashed on the front cover talking about he a murderer. I know that's a lie. Andre do have a bad temper, but with all the tricks and scams I pulled that would cause the average man to kill my ass. Andre never raised a hand to me. If he ever needed a character witness I can attest to that. Now whoring, that's something else."

"So what does the article say, because on the news they only giving bits and pieces."

"The break down is this: They claim that when Andre was seventeen he was overseas with his father who was doing a concert. Supposedly Andre had met this girl who was fifteen. They went back to his hotel room and he raped her. He got scared that she would go to the police so he pushed her over the balcony of his hotel room and she died."

"Yo, that shit sound crazy! So what happened?"

"They locked his ass up. They saying because his father was huge over in Europe that he was able to use his money and fame to get Andre released and the charges dropped."

"Talk about damage control, Andre got a lot to do. Has he ever discussed that with you before?"

"Never. Not to defend him, but I can't see Andre raping nobody. He ain't never been pressed for pussy like that. Too many bitches be throwing it at him."

"I feel you, but people love to believe the worse. So if Andre don't step up and give his side, everybody will be more than happy to run with this story."

As T-Roc was making his way towards the movie set, he saw Chrissie parking her car and thought it would be a good time to play nice since he hadn't had the time lately to stroke her ego. "How are you this morning, beautiful?"

"What do want, T-Roc?"

"That's no way to greet the star of the movie you're doing publicity for."

"You mean the movie you manipulated your way to star in."

T-Roc was surprised by Chrissie's brash attitude. "The logistics of how I got the part didn't seem to matter to you before. What's changed?"

"I'm busy. I don't have time to have this discussion with you."

"I see that you're obviously in a bad mood today so I won't keep you for too long. But I wanted to talk to you about Tyler.

"I should've known. Your two favorite topics—you and Tyler. I heard you the other day using the problems she's having in her relationship with Andre to cozy up to her. You really have no shame."

"Is that jealousy I hear in your voice, Chrissie?"

"Please! I know how diabolical you are. Because Tyler is vulnerable right now, I don't want you to try to use it as an opportunity to weasel your way back into her personal life."

"When and how I get back into Tyler's life is none of your concern."

"While you're being so sure of yourself, don't forget that I know exactly how you manipulated the whole Tyler, Andre and William situation so you could end up with this role, so watch how you speak to me or I can blow your cover wide open."

Before Chrissie could turn around and walk away, T-Roc grabbed her by the back of her neck and pulled her in so close that she could smell the flavor of his Ice Breaker gum. "You seem to forget that it was you who assisted me with my little scam. Don't turn into a woman scorned because I dismissed you from my bed after I got what I wanted and you were of no more use to me. When you're playing with the big boys, you have to learn to suck it up like a man, so don't you ever threaten me because I would hate to break such a lovely neck."

Chrissie saw the coldness in T-Roc's eyes and knew he was dead ass serious. She couldn't believe that there was a time in her life she was so in love with him that she turned on her best friend to please him. When T-Roc originally asked her to help him expose Tyler's personal relationship with Andre to William, she thought it was because he felt slighted that Andre got the starring role in 'Angel' that should've gone to him. He wanted Andre booted from the movie and he figured if William found out that Tyler was carrying on a secret love affair with her costar, especially since he and Tyler were romantically involved at the time, he would oust Andre and it would leave the door wide open for T-Roc to step in. The relationship did explode wide open exactly the way T-Roc expected, but both he and William underestimated Andre's dedication to the movie, and he finished it even though at the time Tyler had ended their relationship.

William felt so terrible that he jumped the gun and gave T-Roc the part before knowing for sure if Andre was backing out, that he offered him the staring role in his next film. It wasn't until after that deal was signed, sealed and delivered that T-Roc burst Chrissie's bubble by telling her that not only did he want to be a movie star but he wanted Tyler, not her, by his side when he got there. Chrissie was devastated.

Soon after, T-Roc did a one-eighty, laid on the charm and convinced Chrissie he was sorry for how he acted and that he was truly over Tyler. But when Chrissie overheard the conversation between T-Roc and Tyler the other day, she realized he still had a sick obsession for Tyler and used her to get one step closer to getting Tyler back. If Tyler and William knew that T-Roc was the one that orchestrated the whole fiasco in the first place, neither one of them would allow him to star in the movie. Chrissie knew she would have to reveal her role and hope that they would forgive her, and it would be worth it to get T-Roc out of all of their lives forever.

"I'm not afraid of your threats," Chrissie snapped.

"Then I underestimated you because that would mean you're a very stupid girl."

"The only person here that's stupid is you. Like hiring Gee to get all your dirt on Andre and take it to the papers. Yes, I know all about your little informant. You had that story planted in today's paper, you evil sonofabitch! How do you think Tyler is going to feel when she finds out that your informant is her black sheep stepbrother, Evan who tried to molest her when she was a little girl?"

T-Roc swallowed hard. "You're fucking crazy. You don't know what you're talking about."

"But I do. I know how to hire investigators too. Your shit is stinking all over the place. I guess you also devised having Evan leave dead rats, roses and blood all over Tyler's trailer too. What, you wanted to drive Tyler to the breaking point so you could rescue her? It's over for you, T-Roc. When I share this information with Tyler she'll never want to see your face again.

T-Roc's mouth hardened around the edges and fire flared in his eyes. "I had no idea that Gee was Tyler's stepbrother or that he had tried to molest her when she was a little girl. And I damn sure didn't tell him to trash her trailer. You cannot fill Tyler's head up with these lies."

Chrissie jerked her body out of T-Roc's grip and straightened up her black blazer before smoothing out her bottled blond ringlets. Once she regained her composure her eyes spit fire right back at T-Roc. "You're done bullying me and manipulating Tyler. I'm not going to fill her head with lies. I'll be simply telling the truth, which she deserves to hear. I will also let her know the role I played in all of this and beg for her forgiveness. Our friendship has been strong and I believe she will forgive me. As for you, I think it's time for you to clean out your dressing room. So don't..." Before Chrissie could complete her thought her cell rang and it was Tyler. "Hello."

"Chrissie, did you see today's paper?" Tyler asked, obviously in tears.

Chrissie stepped a few feet away from T-Roc so he couldn't get a clear listen to their conversation. "Yes, I need to talk to you about that."

"I don't understand why all this bad stuff is happening to us. Andre told me we need to take a break from each other. I love him so much. I don't want to lose him."

"I promise, you won't lose Andre. I know who's behind this."

"What! Who?" Tyler asked with newfound hope in her voice.

"I need to explain in person. I'm on my way to your house." When Chrissie hung up she could see T-Roc still lurking around.

"Chrissie, we need to finish talking."

"No, I have nothing left to say. I'm done and so are you." Chrissie got back in her car ready to divulge all to Tyler.

Chrissie's adrenaline was pumping as she sped down I-405 south on her way to Malibu to see Tyler. Her emotions were a mix of fear that Tyler wouldn't forgive her, shame for playing a role in T-Roc's scheme, and relief that the truth would finally set her free.

When she merged onto I-10 west she was so absorbed with replaying in her mind how she would confess all to Tyler that she didn't notice the black Yukon Denali following her. She got off at her exit and made a left on Heathercliff Road. As she veered around the winding road she was shaken out of her thoughts by the powerful bang to the back of her Mercedes. "What the hell!" Chrissie belted as she looked in her rear view mirror to catch a glimpse of the person who rammed their car into hers. The Denali was so close that it blocked her view to see a thing. Chrissie slammed down on the gas hoping to make a break, but it wasn't meant to be. The Yukon rammed Chrissie's bumper with such force that it pushed her car off the road and pummeling down the cliff, ending in a huge explosion.

Chapter Twelve

Cry For You

From the back of her chauffeur-driven silver Bentley Arnage RL, Tyler glanced out the window to see why the driver was slowing down. There were police and ambulance sirens ringing in the air on the tight road. Tyler could also see a huge smoke-filled cloud looming.

A police officer stopped them and approached their car. "This road is blocked off due to an accident. You'll have to turn around."

"I have Tyler Blake in the car with me. She only lives 5 miles from here," the driver informed the police officer.

"The actress?" the officer asked, peeking his head into the car. His eyes widened. "Ms. Blake, my wife loved you in the movie, 'Angel'."

"Thank you," Tyler said bashfully.

"You can go. It was nice to meet you, Ms. Blake."

Tyler waved goodbye before her driver rolled the window back up. As they drove off, she looked back, hoping that whoever had been in the accident was okay.

"I knew Andre Jackson would be lethal to Tyler's career!" William shouted, tossing the newspaper on the floor.

"William, you need to calm down," Maria said, picking up the paper before closing the door to his office.

"Calm down? The star of my movie is engaged to a murderer and you want me to calm down?"

"*Alleged* murderer. Andre was never convicted of anything."

"How can you defend him?"

"I'm not defending Andre. As a matter of fact I can't stand him. But we don't know for sure that he murdered this young girl. This article is filled with speculation."

"It doesn't matter. Everybody will believe it to be true. Tyler has to end her relationship with Andre immediately. I'll have a spokesperson release a statement."

"Saying what?"

"Basically that the engagement has been called off and the relationship is over."

"You can't do that. Tyler is a grown woman. It's up to her whether she'd rather stay with Andre or not."

"Tyler isn't thinking clearly. She needs me to step in."

"Tyler isn't as fragile as you like to think, William. She's very capable of taking care of herself. She doesn't need you playing hero."

"I'm not trying to play hero," he countered, becoming defensive.

"Like hell you are. Is this about saving Tyler or trying to get back in her bed?"

"What is that supposed to mean?"

"My question was very direct so you know exactly what I mean. Have you been sleeping with me while patiently waiting for the opportunity to rekindle your relationship with my daughter?"

Ring... Ring... Ring

"I have to get this," William said, relieved by the interruption. The call lasted less than a minute, and after he hung up, he sat down on his chair speechless.

"William, who was that?

He was still in shock and took a moment to finally answer Maria. "It's Chrissie."

"What about her?"

"She's dead."

T-Roc and three of his henchmen showed up to the warehouse where he was meeting his informant, Gee. "T-Roc, I've been expecting you. I didn't realize you were bringing company."

"I hope you don't mind."

"Well, you know I prefer to remain anonymous."

"You don't have to worry. These are my most loyal and dedicated men."

"I feel better all ready."

"Excellent. So let's get down to business."

"I'm always interested in doing that. I'm sure you're pleased with the article in today's Los Angeles Times."

"No doubt, as promised you delivered."

"Always do…so I assume you have the other half of my money."

"I don't think you'll need this money, Gee…or should I call you, Evan?"

"Excuse me? I don't know what you're talking about. My name isn't Evan."

"Oh, your name isn't Evan McNeil?" T-Roc could see the color draining from Evan's face although he was trying to put on an unruffled front.

"No it's not," Evan said dubiously.

"Well, I have several reliable sources that say you are."

"Your sources are mistaken, and even if they weren't, why would you care?"

"Because Tyler Blake is very special to me, and from what I understand you're the stepbrother who tried to molest her when she was a little girl."

"Hmm, so this is about Tyler. Didn't you hire me to disrupt her life? But now you're telling me she's so special to you. Pardon me if I find this whole thing amusing."

"But see, I'm not laughing. When I think back on how we met it seems like too much of a coincidence. It's almost as if you came looking for me."

"T-Roc, you're being paranoid."

"It all makes sense now. When I first met you over a year ago, you were lurking around Chrissie's apartment. When I questioned you about it, you claimed that you were a private investigator hired by a suspicious wife who believed her husband was having an affair with Chrissie. You even gave me a business card. But that was all a game and I played right into your hands.

Tyler was always your intended target and I green-lighted your project and paid you on top of that. You put those dead roses and rats in her trailer with 'You're a dead bitch' written in blood." T-Roc's jaw line tensed up and he paused for a moment before he continued. "You're truly a sick motherfucker."

"I'm sick?" Evan sniggered. "You're the one who's obsessed with that bratty, stuck up whore. She ruined my life. My father turned his back on me to play husband to that bitchy ass Maria, and daddy to two pathetic little girls that weren't even his. They never appreciated him. All they wanted was his money. Because of them my mother and I were left to struggle with no financial support from my father. Tyler deserves to suffer and live in misery for each day my mother and I did."

"Your father turning his back on you had nothing to do with you trying to molest a child." T-Roc stated with repulsion dripping from his mouth.

"Don't be fooled by that virtuous face. Tyler was a whore even when she was six years old. She was dying to have sex with me."

T-Roc leaped forward, slamming Evan against the wall as his leather gloved hands held his neck tightly. His henchman we're right behind him ready to make their move. "I wish I could kill you right now with my bare hands. But I promise you, you'll never breathe Tyler's name again after today."

T-Roc released Evan from his grip as two of his henchman stepped in and clenched Evan tightly.

"T-Roc, come on man. Let's talk about this. I got a little worked up but it's not too late to smooth things out."

"Go through every inch of this place and make sure that nothing traces back to me. You did make sure our people went through his crib and car thoroughly, right?" T-Roc asked his third henchman, double checking.

"Yep, they're triple checking as we speak."

"You have someone at my apartment? How do you know where I live?" Evan was trying in vain to break free from the henchmen's grip. He was six feet-two and a solid one hundred-ninety-five pounds, but that was no match for the strapping enforcers dressed in all black.

"How I found out where you live is the least of your worries," T-Roc mocked. "You really can't be a private investigator, because if you were then you would know exactly who I am. And you would have thought twice before ever pissing me off. You're no longer of use to me, Mr. McNeil."

"T-Roc, you can't be serious. We still have so much to accomplish."

"You're right. For one I need for you to sign this letter." T-Roc pulled out an envelope from the inside pocket of his taupe colored linen suit.

"Sign what?" Evan asked trying to read the letter T-Roc laid down on the top of his wooden desk. The man holding Evan's right arm loosened up his grip so Evan could pick up a pen and sign the letter. "I'm not signing anything."

"That's fine. I'll just have Charlie over there cut off each finger, one by one."

Evan eyed Charlie then looked back down at the paper, and without reading it signed the letter.

"You did the right thing, Evan. Since you've been so cooperative, I'll make sure that your untimely death is as painless as possible. Why do you look so shocked? You couldn't have thought it probable that I would let you live."

"T-Roc, you don't have to kill me. I will leave LA and you'll never hear from me or see me again. Our secrets will remain between us, I give you my word."

"You're asking me to trust the word of a child molester... I think I'll pass. Plus, what you just signed was a confession."

"Confession! About what, harassing Tyler?"

"That, and for causing the ill-fated accident that took the life of her best friend, Chrissie."

"What in the hell are you talking about? I didn't kill Chrissie."

"According to this letter you signed, you did. We even had it typed off your home computer. Everything is going to point right back to you."

"But why murder Chrissie?"

"Unfortunately she developed a conscious and planned on telling Tyler everything, including my connection to you. Although if I knew you were a child molester I would've never done business with you in the first place. That's all in the past now, but you will be held accountable for your actions. I'm sure you have a million more questions but I must be going, Tyler is going to need a shoulder to cry on."

"Don't do this!" Evan pleaded, but T-Roc walked out with his right-hand man, leaving Evan with his other two henchmen to finish him off. "T-Roc, I'll be waiting for you to join me in hell!" were the last words T-Roc heard Evan scream before the door slammed behind him.

***I wonder what's taking Chrissie so** long,* Tyler thought as she dialed Chrissie's cell number for the third time to no avail. It was once again going straight to voicemail and Tyler was restless, wanting to know who was behind leaking the information about Andre.

After slamming her phone down she heard the doorbell ringing and ran to get it, thinking it was Chrissie. "Not you two. I really don't have time for this," Tyler said, frowning at her mother and William before walking off and leaving the door ajar.

"Darling, we need to speak to you. It's important," Maria said as she and William entered the marble foyer, closing the door behind them. They followed Tyler, who was sitting on the couch in the living room dialing a phone number. "Who are you calling?"

"Mother, it's none of your business. But if you must know, I'm calling Chrissie. She has something very important to tell me. That's who I thought was at the door, but of course I was wrong. She was supposed to be here over an hour ago," Tyler said, continuing to dial her number.

"Put the phone down." Tyler ignored William until he came and took the phone from her hand and hung it up.

"William, what is wrong with you?"

"I don't know how to tell you this…"

"Tell me what?"

William swallowed hard trying to figure out the right words to say but knowing there were none. "Chrissie is dead."

"That's not funny, you're lying. Give me that phone." Tyler ripped her phone out of William's hand and started dialing Chrissie's number again. Once again it went straight to voice mail, but that didn't deter her. She dialed over and over again, pressing each number harder and harder as if it would make a difference. "Damn it, Tyler, she's not going to answer!" Maria yelled.

"No-o-o-o-o!" Tyler screamed, throwing the phone across the room. She fell down on the cold white marble floor and let the tears fall.

William bent down and held her. "I'm so sorry," he whispered.

"What happened?"

"She was in a car accident."

"Where?"

"On Heathercliff Road."

"Oh my goodness. She must have been on her way to see me. I passed that accident on my way home. I had no idea it was Chrissie. I don't understand. First Andre now Chrissie. It seems to be one tragedy after another," Tyler said, shaking her head. "You know she was on her way over to tell me who leaked that story about Andre. I hope she wasn't rushing to get here and lost control of her car. I would feel horrible."

"Tyler, you can't blame yourself. It was a terrible accident."

"But, William, it was right near my house and she died never being able to tell me who is behind trying to ruin Andre."

Chantal was snuggling under her soft pink Frette silk comforter with a glass of champagne in her hand preparing to read the article about Andre one more time before going to sleep, when her phone rang. "Hello," she answered, not bothering to look at her caller ID.

"Am I disturbing you?"

Chantal slit her eyes at the receiver not believing Ian was on the other end of the phone. "You have some nerve calling me after the way you played me out at that event."

"Ma, you played yourself. I didn't have nothing to do with that."

"Why the fuck you call me if all you spitting is slick ass lines?"

"I read that article in the paper today about Andre and I was checking to see if you were alright."

"Oh, so you're concerned about me? You weren't too concerned when I was sitting up in jail for three days."

"Damn right I left you in jail. I was mad as hell that you put Tyler on blast by using confidential information I shared with you. That was some straight nonsense that I didn't appreciate. I was a presenter at that event, and not only did you embarrass yourself but you embarrassed me too. You need to dead this fixation you have with Tyler because it got you acting a fool."

"My fixation...you were sniffing around her like a lost puppy when it's obvious she has moved on to the next man."

"Listen, I'm not about to explain my relationship with Tyler to you."

"See, that's where you got it twisted, booboo. There is no *relationship* between you and Tyler," Chantal scoffed. "It's clear you ain't over her, and so you want to call my phone pestering me on my first night back home and being able to sleep in the comfort of my bed after my stint in that filthy ass jail cell."

"You know what? Maybe it was a mistake calling you."

"Maybe you're right."

"Goodnight, Chantal."

"Goodnight!" Chantal said, slamming the phone down. She was livid when she got off the phone with Ian. She couldn't decide if she was angry because of the hostile words they just exchanged or because she missed him so much. Chantal gulped the rest of her champagne down and turned off the lights, falling asleep with that very question on her mind.

Shari was looking forward to seeing Jalen. He came into town for a game the team had against the Chicago Bulls. He suggested they go out, but Shari convinced him they should stay in. It wasn't that difficult once she told him about the home cooked meal she was preparing. Besides an exceptional blow job, there was no better way to a man's heart than with some slap-your-mama fried chicken, baked macaroni cheese, collard greens, cinnamon sweet yams and homemade biscuits. Shari had only cooked this meal one other time in her life, and that was when she was trying to lock down Alex's father. The meal definitely worked, because soon after, they were living together and he was telling her everyday how much he loved her and that he wanted her to be the mother of his first born child.

Shari was ecstatic to carry his seed, since at the time he was the new up and coming hot young actor. She couldn't get pregnant fast enough. But soon she realized the once hot actor's career was colder than a tray of ice cubes and by then it was too late. Shari was eight months pregnant, and she also found out that not only did he already have two crumb snatchers by two different women, but that another girl who lived down the street from her was also pregnant with his child.

The stress hit Shari so hard that her doctor had to put her on bed rest for the duration of her pregnancy. Needless to say, her baby daddy didn't even stick around for the delivery of their son, and since his career was over before it started, it wasn't even worth taking him to court for child support. Like Chantal told her, you can't get water from a dry well. That was a hard knock lesson Shari had to learn and she planned on never making that mistake again.

But lately, an optimistic cloud was floating above her head. She couldn't help but think of what Chantal said about her spaceship maybe finally coming in. Could Jalen be the millionaire husband she'd been praying for? Would a man finally step in her life and hold it down for her and her son? These were all questions Shari had, and hoped they'd be answered soon.

As she made the final touches to her deliciously cooked meal, she reasoned that once Jalen got a taste of her food and a taste of what was between her legs, the deal would be sealed and she'd be taking "Griffin" on as her last name.

"Coming," Shari whistled as she heard Jalen knocking on her front door. *And so the games begin,* she thought to herself.

Chapter Thirteen

Don't Be Cruel

Tyler woke up early the next morning still wearing the same clothes she had on yesterday. She remembered her mother and William staying by her side until she cried herself to sleep. It still didn't seem real to her that Chrissie was gone and never coming back.

On her way up the stairs to take a shower and put on some clean clothes the doorbell rang. She wasn't in the mood to see anybody, but with so much going on something told her to answer. When she opened the door two men were standing outside. "Can I help you?"

"Yes, Ms. Blake, I'm Detective Reilly and this is my partner, Detective Richards," he said as they both flashed their badges. "We're sorry to bother you, but we wanted to ask you a few questions."

"Do I need to have my attorney present?"

"Of course you can if you would like, but we don't think it's necessary."

"What are the questions pertaining to?"

"Chrissie Nichols."

"Oh, please come in."

"Thank you, Ms. Blake."

"I apologize if I came off a bit unreceptive. With Chrissie's accident and so many other things going on I'm not myself."

"No need to apologize. I know there must be a lot of pressure being a big movie star and all. We'll try not to take up too much of your time."

"No, please, whatever you need. Chrissie was like a sister to me."

"Ms. Blake, I'm sorry you had to get the door. I was in the middle of doing some cleaning," the maid explained

"Don't worry about it, Deanna. These detectives wanted to speak with me about Chrissie's accident."

"That's so sad. I'm still in shock. Chrissie was a very nice woman. Can I get you gentleman anything?"

"We're fine."

"How about you, Ms. Blake?"

"A glass of orange juice would be great."

Deanna went to the kitchen while Tyler led the detectives to the living room.

"Please have a seat."

The officers sat down on the pristine white mohair velvet couch across from Tyler. "Ms. Blake—"

"Call me Tyler."

Detective Reilly began talking as his partner took out his pen and pad to take notes. "Tyler, we have reason to believe that your friend Chrissie's accident was actually murder."

"What, who would want to kill Chrissie?"

"Do you know a man by the name of Evan McNeil?"

Hearing that name made Tyler feel that they were resurrecting the devil. "Yes, that's my stepbrother. But what does Evan have to do with this?"

"Here you go, Ms. Blake," Deanna said, leaning down to place the glass on the high-gloss custom white coffee table.

"Evan McNeil was discovered last night dead in a black Yukon Denali with what seems to be a self inflicted gunshot wound to the head. The front of the truck was damaged, and we believe it was the vehicle used to drive your friend off the road. We won't know for sure until we run tests to match the paint. Apparently he also left a suicide note and forensics is checking to see if the signature is a match."

"Oh, Ms. Blake, I'm so sorry. I didn't mean to spill the juice," Deanna said with her hands shaking. The detectives both reached in their pockets and pulled out their handkerchiefs, cleaning up the small mess. "I'll bring you another glass."

"That's okay." Tyler stood up, clutching her arms and feeling as if the walls were caving in on her. "In the letter, did he say why he killed Chrissie?"

"Supposedly she found out he was out to get you and trashed your trailer. Did that happen?"

"Yes, somebody wrote in blood that I was a dead bitch. That was Evan?"

"We believe so. He probably got scared that she would blow the whistle on him and decided to kill her. But it seems his conscience kicked in and the guilt was eating him up, so he also ended up killing himself."

"It's all my fault."

"No, Ms. Blake, you can't blame yourself. Evan McNeil was evidently a very disturbed man," Detective Reilly said. "But it would be helpful if you could explain what Mr. McNeil had against you."

"When I was a little girl, Evan tried to molest me. His father caught him and threw him out of the house. They never reconciled and Evan always blamed me. About ten years ago he showed up at our house and he threatened me and my mother, but I never believed he would follow through on it. Now my best friend is dead because of that monster. I wonder if he's responsible for digging up that information on Andre and leaking it to the press." Tyler wondered out loud.

"Excuse me?"

"Sorry, I'm thinking out loud. Chrissie was on her way to see me before the accident. There was an article in the paper yesterday about my fiancé, Andre Jackson, and Chrissie told me she knew who leaked the story. But of course she never had a chance to tell me. I can't help but wonder if it was Evan."

"We'll check into that. It would make sense."

"I'm glad this madness is making sense to one of us because it's totally sending my life into a tailspin. Detectives, if you don't have anymore questions, I really need some time alone."

"Of course, but we will keep you posted on any new developments."

"Thank you. Deanna, can you please show the detectives to the door?"

Deanna obliged and Tyler immediately headed to the kitchen and opened up a new bottle of champagne. After her third glass, she felt that champagne was no longer enough and desperately wanted something stronger to numb her pain.

When Chantal woke up in the morning she decided that it was time for her to go home to Chicago. She was beginning to wear her welcome out in the city of stars and yearned for a break.

She pulled out her Louis Vuitton Damier Azur luggage collection and began packing. After finishing, she slipped on a pair of shapely fitting Genetic jeans with a cream colored cropped cape and Devi Kroell python boots. She pulled her honey blond locks back loosely in a pony tail, dabbed on some lip gloss, put on her gold sculptured, hand-polished acetate frame shades and headed to the LAX airport.

"Shari, I'm in the car headed towards the airport and I need you to pick me up when I arrive in Chicago."

"Of course. But girl, what made you decide to finally come home?"

"For one, I miss Melanie, and pretty soon my parents are going to think she's their daughter if I don't go get her. And two, this Hollywood lifestyle isn't for me. It's been nothing but drama since my arrival. Girl, even a scheming ass bitch like me needs to fall back and take a break every now and then."

"I heard that. I can't wait to see you. Call me and let me know what time you'll be landing and I'll be there."

Chantal was looking forward to going back to a place that everybody loved her despite her flaws.

T-Roc had just finished up his one hour morning ritual on the Vision Fitness X6600 HRT, when a call came in. He gulped down half of his vitamin water and used the towel to wipe away the sweat from his face before answering the phone. "Hello," he answered, not exhibiting any indication that he had just put in a strenuous workout.

"Hi, T-Roc, this is William."

"William, how are you?"

"Not good. I don't know if you heard, but Chrissie Nichols was in a fatal car accident yesterday."

"Dear God, are you serious?"

"Yes. We're having her funeral Monday. Of course you're more than welcome to come. So instead of leaving Monday to go to New York to finish filming, we're leaving Wednesday."

"I understand. How's Tyler holding up?"

"Not good. She's taking it very hard."

"I can imagine. Chrissie was such a lovely woman. I can't believe a tragedy like this happened to her. You truly have to be grateful for each day."

"You're so right, T-Roc. I was saying the same thing myself. I have a few other calls to make, but if you'll like to attend the funeral I'll have my assistant call you later on with the details."

"I'd appreciate that, William, and thanks for calling."

T-Roc walked in the bathroom, turned on the faucet and splashed water across his face. He then stared at his reflection in the mirror. He had surprised himself with the lengths he was going through to have Tyler. He felt he had done her and the world a favor by getting rid of Evan, but having Chrissie killed left him with remorse. *If only she would have stayed silent and not threatened to expose everything to Tyler,* T-Roc kept saying to himself. But it was too late. Chrissie was dead and there was no bringing her back. He knew he couldn't dwell on it any further because all it would do was drive him mad. *What you won't do, do for love*—But what type of love is this?

"Ms. Blake, there is someone here to see you," Deanna said outside of Tyler's bedroom door. Tyler was starting to wake up from her champagne induced sleep and wasn't quite alert.

"Send them away," she said with her voice slurring.

"The gentleman said it's very important. He needs to see you."

"Who is it?"

"A Mr. Ian Addison."

"Damn, I don't feel like seeing him." *But knowing Ian, if I don't hear what he has to say then he'll keep coming back until we talk,* Tyler said to herself. "Deanna, tell him to wait and I'll be down in fifteen minutes."

"No problem."

Tyler dragged herself out of bed and took a couple of migraine Excedrin before getting in the steam shower. By the time she let the hot water drench her body, put on a pair of sweats and tank top, her headache was beginning to subside. When she got downstairs Ian was staring out the vast windows watching the waves. "It's beautiful, isn't it?"

"Tyler, I didn't hear you come down. But yeah, you're right, this view is incredible. I need me a place like this to get away and unwind. It's so peaceful."

"Tell me about it. Now if I can only get my front gates fixed then maybe I can have some real peace, since my home has become a revolving door."

"I'm sorry. I shouldn't have popped up like this."

"It's okay. I'll admit at first I didn't want to see you, but now that I have, it's nice."

"I guess that's a good thing."

"I would say so. How did you find out where I live anyway?"

"Tyler, this is my town. What can't I find out?"

"Too bad you couldn't have found out that someone was going to kill Chrissie."

"Kill? I thought Chrissie died in a car accident."

"That's what it seemed like at first, but early this morning a couple of detectives came to see me, and it wasn't an accident. My stepbrother, Evan purposely ran Chrissie off the road."

"What?"

"Yeah. I don't feel like rehashing everything, but basically he was seeking revenge against me, and Chrissie found out about it. He killed her to shut her up, and now both of them are dead."

"Tyler, I'm so sorry. I know how much you loved Chrissie, but please don't blame yourself."

Ian wrapped his long muscular arms around Tyler, making her feel secure. In her heart she wished it was Andre that was doing so, but he still hadn't reached out to her or returned any of her calls.

"I also wanted to apologize for happened with Chantal at the charity event," he added, stepping back and releasing Tyler from his embrace.

"You're not responsible for Chantal's actions."

"I know, but I should've never told her about our past."

"Why did you anyway?"

"There were so many feelings I had built up and I wanted to get them off my chest. Chantal was there to listen."

"Out of all the women, you would confide in the one who hates me the most."

"Hated by few, but loved by so many."

"So you think."

"Look at you. Tyler Blake, this huge superstar."

"You're one to talk. You're like, what, one of the biggest basketball players in the world. You're on every freaking billboard in LA."

"Maybe so, but you're a movie star. When we first met, you always told me you wanted to be a star."

"I remember. You made me feel like my dream was a bad joke."

"It wasn't that I thought your dream was a joke, I was jealous."

"Jealous of what?"

"That if you stepped out there and pursued stardom that you would make it and I would lose you. That was my biggest fear, but I ended up losing you anyway. What happened with us Tyler? Why couldn't we make it work?"

"We were both so young and caused each other too much pain. We weren't good for one another. Our relationship was so volatile. And after all these years, I still can't seem to get it right."

"Neither can I. Any day now I'll be signing my divorce papers, and I don't know what I'll do next."

"I'm sorry your marriage didn't work, especially since you all have a child together."

"I heard that you have a little one too."

"My son, Christian. I miss him so much. I'm excited because we're going to spend a couple of weeks together while I'm filming in New York."

"That's great. When are you leaving?"

"We were supposed to leave Monday, but we're having Chrissie's funeral, so Wednesday."

"We have a game against the Knicks on Friday. I would love if you and your little man would come and cheer me on."

"I think he would like that, and so would I."

"I hope you don't mind me asking, but what is going on between you and Andre?"

Tyler put her head down. She realized that she somewhat opened the door for this line of questioning, but it was still hard to talk about. "Andre said he needed space, which technically means we broke up. But I'm hoping he'll come to his senses and realize we belong together, because I love him so much."

"I can see it in your eyes. He'll be back. He'd be crazy not to."

"I pray that you're right, because my heart can't take another blow."

Shari was right on time picking Chantal up from the airport. After Chantal tipped the skycap for putting her luggage in the back of Shari's classic silver metallic Lexus LX, she sat in the passenger seat. "Girl, it's so good to see you," Chantal smiled.

"It's good to see you too. You looking all Hollywood with those bad ass shades on. Are those Louis Vuitton?"

"You know it, sweetie. But don't stress, I picked you up a pair too because they don't sell them at all the stores, only a selected few."

"You my bitch, that's what's up," Shari said as the two ladies gave each other their signature pinky shake. "So what you trying to do? You hungry? You want to stop at Charlie Trotter's?"

"Let's go tomorrow. Right now I want to go straight to my parents' house. I miss Melanie like crazy. I have to see my baby girl."

"I hear that. So what's been going on with you? Did you ever speak to Ian?"

"Girl, yes. That motherfucker called me on some bullshit."

"What you mean?'

"Well you know he didn't bail me out when I got locked up over that Tyler drama, and then when he did call, he had the nerve to say it was my own damn fault for playing myself. Shit, I didn't need him to tell me that. If that was his only words of encouragement he should've never dialed my number."

"I feel you, but I thought you were digging him."

"I was—I mean I am—but I'm tired of catching feelings for these dudes that's still chasing after fucking Tyler Blake. These cats acting like she the only bad bitch in this entire world—enough already."

"Oka-a-a-ay. I mean she cute, but it ain't that deep. So what you going to do?"

"Put him on pause until he snap out of his hallucination. See, I know Andre has put it on Tyler right and she isn't leaving him no time soon. That bitch would walk through fire first. You see how he sent me postal. When Ian become conscious and grasp that Tyler now belongs to Andre, he'll be back. And as fine as he is, I'll be more than willing to give him another chance to make it right. Enough about me, what about you? Any fresh meat in your life?"

"Actually, I'm still tenderizing that meat from Jalen," Shari said, winking her eye.

"I knew that relationship had a lot of potential to it. So you still going strong with the eighty-million-dollar rookie. That's a good look."

"I think so. You know after dealing with that closet homo, Chris Duncan episode I was looking at all men sideways."

"Shit, me too. It took me a minute to get over that fine ass football player being a switch hitter. But fuck him, because that Jalen is a cutie."

"Yeah, but he live in LA, and unless two people are really devoted it's hard to make a long distance relationship work. So, girl, I'm chilling, taking it day by day. I'm not going to start picking out a wedding dress just yet. When the time is right, if it's meant to be then I'll get that sign."

"You got that right. That sign will come in a little black box with about ten carats weighing it down. Damn, it seem like you got here fast as hell," Chantal said as they pulled up to her parents' small two-story brick house on the tree-lined street. "Don't think you're about to pull off, because I need you to help me with my bags."

"I got you."

The ladies carried Chantal's heavy luggage to the front entrance and rang the doorbell. Nobody answered so Chantal opened the screen door and knocked. She could hear Melanie running and then the door opened.

"It's Mommy!" Melanie screamed, giving Chantal a big hug and kiss.

"Oh, baby, I'm so happy to see you! You've gotten so big. Look how pretty you are." Melanie paused and twirled around, showing off her hot pink Juicy couture jogging suit with matching bows in her two French braids. "You are too cute, sweetie."

"And grown, just like her momma," Shari added.

"Mommy, follow me in the kitchen. I have a surprise for you."

Chantal dropped her luggage, leaving Shari to carry them as she followed Melanie.

"Look who's here, Daddy, it's Mommy," Melanie said brightly as Andre sat at the kitchen table.

"Andre, I'm surprised to see you here."

"I'm surprised to see you too."

"If you think I followed you on some stalking type mess, I didn't."

"No, I don't think that at all."

"Good. So how long have you been here?"

"For a few days, visiting my little princess," Andre said, putting Melanie in a bear hug. Melanie laughed so hard and it put a smile on Chantal's face seeing her so happy to be with her dad.

"Isn't this cute," Shari said, coming into the kitchen. "Andre, I didn't know you were here. I didn't see your car out front."

"I had my driver drop me off and I'll call him when I'm ready to be picked up. With press hounding me, I try my best not to let them be able to track my every move."

"I feel you. The life of a superstar, it never stops," Shari giggled. "Well, I'm outta here, so call me tomorrow, Chantal so we can hang out."

"Will do."

"Bye, Andre, bye Melanie."

"Bye, Auntie Shari. Tell Alex I said hi."

"I will." Shari let her self out and Chantal had a sit at the table with Andre and Melanie.

"Where my parents' at?"

"Grandma's upstairs reading the Bible and Grandpa is at work."

"Some things never change. So how much longer are you going to be here, Andre?"

"I'm actually about to head out in a few."

"I hope you're not leaving because I showed up."

"No it's not like that."

"So you wouldn't mind giving me and Melanie a ride home?"

"Would you, Daddy."

"Of course." Melanie gave her dad a big kiss.

"Great. I'm going upstairs to speak with my mother and I'll be down in a few."

Chantal walked out of the kitchen and upstairs, bypassing the same floral couch with matching loveseat, the old wooden table that was filled with pictures from when Chantal was a child all the way up to her high school graduation. The wall was decorated with pictures of Melanie, and one that had her, Andre and Melanie when they were a family. When Chantal reached the middle step it still squeaked like it did when she was in high school. It made her laugh to herself because when she would stay out late and miss her curfew, she would always forget to skip that step and it would wake her mother up, and she would get caught. *How so many things changes and so much stays the same,* Chantal thought to herself.

Chantal lightly knocked on her mother's door, "Who is it?" Mrs. Morgan said in a gentle voice.

"It's me, Ma, Chantal."

"Come on in. I was just finishing up my reading for the night." Mrs. Morgan closed up her Bible and set it down on the nightstand next to her bed. "Come give me a hug, When did you get here?"

"A few minutes ago. Shari dropped me off."

"Is Shari here her sweet self?"

"No, she's gone, but you'll see her before I leave."

"How long you staying?"

"I'm not sure, but I missed Melanie so much and it was time for me to come home."

"I guess you and Andre was both missing Melanie. You saw him downstairs, didn't you?"

"Yes I did, and it felt so good to see Melanie happy. She's always been a daddy's little girl."

"Hmm hum, just like her mother."

Chantal sat down next to her mother on the hand-quilted blanket. "I know I haven't told you this, but thank you so much for taking care of Melanie while I've been dealing with all my drama."

"You don't have to thank me, that's my granddaughter. I would do anything for her."

"I know you would, but still, you don't have to."

"Yes I do. I owe it to that child because somewhere I went wrong with you," Mrs. Morgan said solemnly.

"What do you mean?"

"You know what I mean."

"No, Ma, I don't."

"Chantal, look at you... running over people with your car, going to jail, scheming and manipulating. I never thought I would raise a child to be that type of a person. Somewhere I failed you, and hopefully, by the grace of God, I will find salvation through Melanie."

"Ma, you're still angry that I took that seven-thousand-dollars when I left here on my graduation. That's what this is about. I told you I was sorry, I even tried to give you the money back but you wouldn't accept it."

"Dear child, it isn't about the money. God always takes care of his children. He may not give you what you want, but he always gives you what you need and it's always right on time, so your father and I were never without. You didn't steal that money from me, you stole it from yourself. And until you realize that true wealth in this world is not from this," she rubbed her fingers together indicating money, "But from what's in this," she pointed to her heart, "Then you'll forever be a slave in your own world."

Chantal was speechless. She had heard the many sermons growing up from her mother, but this one struck a chord. With all the sex, lies and videotapes, what had she gained? Andre never married her, she was still alone, and although Melanie was her greatest achievement, what else had she accomplished in life? She had no career and her biggest goal still remained being a superstar's wife.

Chapter Fourteen

Can't Make You Love Me

When Tyler arrived home from Chrissie's funeral, the first thing she did was go in the kitchen and gulp down more than half a bottle of champagne from the bottle before pouring what was left over into a glass. The paparazzi were relentless in their pursuit of her, and it was wearing Tyler down. She hoped they would at least respect her privacy while mourning her best friend, but they didn't care. With the story of her stepbrother, Evan being responsible for Chrissie's death now trickling down, combined with all the questions surrounding Andre, the media was having a field day. Everyday Tyler's face was splashed across some newspaper or magazine, and the headline on every entertainment news program.

"Tyler, do you really need to be drinking?" her mother asked as her and William sat down in the living room.

"Yes, I do. And although I do appreciate both of your concern, there is no need for you to stay here and baby sit me."

"We're not babysitting, we're just making sure you're okay."

"William, if you're worried that I won't be ready to go to New York on Wednesday to work, you're wrong. I'll be fine."

"You say that, but I'm becoming somewhat concerned about your drinking."

"Me too," her mother chimed in.

"I'm just going through a rough time right now. With Chrissie and Andre, then the whole Evan situation, I need something to calm my nerves. But I have it under control." Tyler caught her mother and William giving each other a sly look. "What are you guys, like my parents' now? I mean really, it seems that overnight you all have turned into some couple. Is that what's going on, my ex-lover and mother are now a serious item—and you wonder why I drink."

"Tyler, I know you're stressed. The whole Evan coming back for revenge took me by complete surprise. I knew he was vile but not to that extent. And Chrissie, that's devastating, but I believe your anxiety is because of Andre. I tried to warn you that he was no good for you. I know his type. He'll cause you nothing but heartbreak. It's better that he is out of your life now instead of you having some kids with him and he end up abandoning you later," said Maria.

"Can you please just shut up?" Tyler's demand made Maria's mouth drop.

"Ms. Blake, there is a Mr. T-Roc at the gate for you."

"Thank goodness the gate is finally working correctly," Tyler said to no one in particular. "Yes, Deanna, let him in. Now the two of you can get out. T-Roc can baby sit me while you all go off and do whatever it is you do."

"Tyler, dear, you don't even like T-Roc."

"Mother, once again you're wrong, but then anybody is better than watching the two of you sit up in my face. You all's relationship is absolutely disgusting."

"You're drunk," William said, grabbing the glass out of Tyler's hand."

"Whether I'm drunk or not is beside the point. It doesn't change a thing. And besides, aren't you still married, William?"

"As a matter of fact my divorce went through a month ago." Maria's face instantly lit up upon hearing the news.

"Don't get any ideas, Mother. William likes his women young." Tyler patted William on his shoulder in a patronizing way. "You're a little bit too long in the tooth for him."

"William, I think we ought to go now," Maria said, grabbing her purse.

"I'm sure you do."

"We can't leave her like this."

"Can I help?" All three of them turned simultaneously and stared a T-Roc. "Your maid let me in. Is everything okay? I feel like I just walked in on something."

"Everything is fine. William and I were just leaving."

"Don't let the door hit you on your way out, Mother."

"I think I should stay here with her, Maria. She doesn't look well."

"William, she's drunk. She'll be fine. Besides, T-Roc is here. He can take care of her now."

"She's right. I'll make sure that Tyler is okay." William looked at T-Roc and then back at Tyler.

"William, I'll be fine. I'm headed to bed anyway. I need the rest."

"Okay, I'll call and check up on you later on." William kissed Tyler on the cheek before leaving.

Tyler sat back down on the couch relieved that both William and her mother were gone.

"I guess you're taking Chrissie's death pretty hard," T-Roc said as he sat down across from Tyler.

"I guess so." Tyler let out a yawn as the champagne and sleepless nights began taking a toll on her body.

"Tyler, you know I'm here if you need me."

"That seems to be everyone's favorite line, but the person I need to hear it from the most is nowhere around."

"I'm assuming you're speaking of Andre."

"Of course."

"When is the last time you spoke to him?"

"It feels like a lifetime ago."

"He hasn't called you since news spread about Chrissie's death?"

"No, he hasn't. He sent some flowers, but when I called to thank him his voicemail picked up. He still doesn't want to speak to me. Andre and I have been through so much. I didn't think anything could come between us. Now, I don't know if anything will bring us back. I wish I had something to take all the pain away."

"I figured you did. Here, I brought something for you." T-Roc handed Tyler a small package of white pills.

"What are they? And don't say natural herbal pills."

"There not harmful. They'll make you feel relaxed. But don't take more than one at a time."

Tyler immediately popped one in her mouth and washed it down with the rest of her champagne.

"In the future, don't take it with champagne. It's powerful enough on its own. All you need is the pill." T-Roc desperately wanted to hold Tyler, kiss her, but he didn't want her under these conditions. When they made love again he wanted Tyler to want him just as much as he wanted her.

The sun was beginning to set as Chantal sat outside by the pool watching Andre and Melanie play catch. It was an unseasonably warm day as spring was approaching, and Melanie was taking full advantage.

"Daddy, get the ball," Melanie said after tossing the ball in the bushes. Only Melanie could get Andre to get down on his hands and knees in his velour Sean John sweat suit with fresh out of the box sneakers to look for a ball. "You found it! You found it!" Melanie jumped up and down after Andre lifted his arm in the air with ball in hand.

"Melanie, it's time for you to go inside and have dinner. Abby cooked your favorite."

"But, Mommy, I want to keep playing with Daddy."

"We can play tomorrow, princess. Go inside to eat. You need to be strong if you want to play with me," he said, tickling her tummy.

"Okay, Daddy," Melanie giggled uncontrollably, and then Andre picked her up and carried her up to the house. Afterwards he walked back out and sat down outside with Chantal.

"Melanie really adores Abby."

"I would think so. She's been her nanny since she was practically a baby."

"Wow, it's been that long?"

"I know. I can't believe Melanie is going on six. It seems like yesterday she was barely walking. When you think about how fast time flies it makes you appreciate life so much more. Like having you spend time with us for the last few days have been incredible. I've never seen Melanie so happy."

"I know and she deserves it. She's been through some pretty tough times with us."

"Who you telling? We've had a few crazy times, me trying to run you over being the craziest."

"Chantal, I'm sorry about that."

"Why are you sorry?"

"Because I know I drove you to it. You didn't deserve to be left at the church on our wedding day. That was cruel and I'll always feel ashamed about that."

"I can't believe what you're saying. Where is this coming from?"

"I've always felt guilty for what led up to that night and I never wanted to see you spend the rest of your life in jail. But for the last couple of weeks I've been doing a lot of soul searching and getting my priorities in order. And family is of the utmost importance. I'm trying to make things right."

"Does this have anything to do with that article that was in the paper?"

Andre looked off in the distance for a moment. "That was definitely an eye opener. When your past comes back to haunt you it can remind you of the mistakes you continue to make in the present. I'm still trying to figure all that out and maybe one day I'll be ready to explain to you what happened that night."

Chantal put her hand on Andre's hand. "You don't have to. No matter what anybody says, I know in my heart you're not a murderer."

"Thank you, Chantal, I needed to hear that, but I have to be getting back to my hotel. I'm starving."

"Stay for dinner. Abby cooked enough for all of us."

"I don't know…"

"She made creamy Cajun shrimp linguine."

"I guess I could stay a little while longer," Andre said with a smile.

By the time Chantal and Andre came back inside from talking, Melanie had finished her dinner. They both gave her a kiss goodnight before Abby took her upstairs to prepare Melanie's bath for bedtime.

"Go have a seat in the dining room."

Andre got comfortable in one of the red leather armchairs while Chantal fixed his plate and poured him a glass of Chateau Margaux.

"This looks delicious," Andre said as Chantal placed the plate on the glass top butterfly table.

"Chantal, I put Melanie to bed. She was exhausted so I'll be heading home now. I'll see you in the morning. Have a good evening, Mr. Jackson," Abby said from the foyer.

"You too," Andre replied as Chantal let Abby out.

"Andre, have some more wine. I'm going upstairs to check on Melanie. I'll be back in a few." Chantal peeked in Melanie's room and she looked like a little angel sleeping so peacefully. She closed the door and went to her bedroom. With Melanie fast asleep and Abby gone for the evening, Chantal felt it was time to make her move.

She took off her grey cashmere dress and slipped on a seductive black mesh embroidery bra and panty set with a delicate floral pattern, oversized removable center bow with a diamanté brooch. For the final touch, she decorated her freshly French manicured feet with black chandelier sandals with dripping, sparkling gemstones. She sprayed perfume on her neck, stomach, thighs and the back of her legs, and then released the clip from her hair and tossed her head down before letting it cascade across her delicate shoulder bones. Chantal sized herself quickly in the full-length mirror and made her way downstairs to capture her prey.

Andre was so preoccupied pouring himself another glass of wine that he didn't hear Chantal come back down until she was right up on him.

"How do I look?" Chantal asked, knowing she was putting the "d" in delicious. "Andre, you can close your mouth. It's not like you've never seen me in my bra and panties before," she said flirtatiously.

"I don't know what to say."

"You don't have to say a word. There's no need to talk for what we're about to do." Chantal glided closer, leaning over sideways so Andre could take in every ample curve on her body.

The outline trace of her figure reflected an endless curl. She then reached her hand down, placing it provocatively on the crotch of his pants.

"You need to stop."

"Baby, if you're worried about Melanie, don't be, she's sound asleep. It's just me and you... like how it used to be back in the day."

"That's the thing. We're not back in the day, we're in the present," Andre said, removing Chantal's hand from his crotch.

"What are you doing?" Chantal's look of confusion was genuine. She didn't understand what was going on with Andre.

"I have to stop doing this."

"Doing what?"

"Giving you these mixed signals."

"Don't even go there. I know when a man is interested in me, especially you. You want me, Andre, and don't try to deny it or say I'm getting mixed signals, because it's bullshit."

"I know you believe what you're saying and that's why I need to check myself. Chantal, these last few days have been great, and I am interested in you as the mother of my child, and hopefully one day as a friend."

Chantal felt as if the wind had been knocked out of her. Was she so hard up that she imagined Andre wanting to make love to her? "What about that talk regarding family and priorities?"

"We are family. We share a beautiful daughter together. I'll always love you for that. But it isn't a romantic love."

"Let me guess, that's the love you have for Tyler."

"Yes, it is."

"Then why are you here playing house with us and not with the woman you claim to love?"

"Do you really want me to have this conversation with you?"

Chantal thought hard about what Andre was asking. His underlining question was if she was ready to hear and accept the truth. "I'm ready, but let me sit down for this."

Before he began speaking, Andre rubbed his fingers over his mouth like he always did when something was heavy on his mind.

"Honestly, I never thought it was possible to love a woman as much as I love Tyler. So much so, that everyday I worry my past mistakes will make me a disappointment to her and she'll wake up and say she doesn't love me anymore. That makes me afraid so I'm running from her instead of to her."

"But, Andre, Tyler is no angel. I told you about her relationship with T-Roc and Ian, so she's made mistakes too. And don't tell me she denied that mess."

"No, she didn't deny it. Tyler never pretended to be perfect, it's just that in my eyes she was. When she admitted it was true it cut so deep because I never wanted to believe she had a life before me. I wanted to believe her life didn't begin until she met me."

"Andre, I'm confused. You sound crazy right now. Of course Tyler had a life before you, and you damn sure had a life before her."

"That was the problem. I was so caught up in my life with Tyler that for a moment I didn't care about the life I had in the past. It wasn't until I accepted she had a history with T-Roc and Ian that made a difference in her life that I had to remember that I had people that made a difference in mine too."

Chantal was starting to understand where Andre was coming from but the clarity was painful. "When you say the people who made a difference, you're talking about Melanie?" Chantal paused for a second waiting for Andre to respond, but his silence answered her question. "Damn, Andre, you was so caught up in that broad that you forgot about your own daughter."

"Not that I forgot, but damn sure took her for granted. That's what I meant about the importance of family and prioritizing. But I promise I'll never take Melanie for granted again."

"Do you think you and Tyler will get back together?"

"In my heart we've never been apart."

"Can I ask you a question? And swear that you'll tell me the truth."

"We seem to be having a meeting of the minds right now. If you want the truth, I'll give it to you."

154

"Why do you love Tyler so much? Why is she the one you want to make your wife?"

Andre let out a deep sigh as he folded his hands, resting his arms on the table. "You're not holding no punches, huh, ma?"

"Nah, I figure this might be my only chance to hear the truth, and I want to know."

"I believe I fell in love with Tyler the first moment I laid eyes on her."

"You can't be serious."

"I really am, but once I got past that initial infatuation, I became captivated by Tyler because at first glance, she appears to be this delicate flower that's supposed to sit there and be pretty. But when you zoom in it's clear there are so many more layers than meets the eye."

"So she has layers. That's why you fell in love with her and you want to make her your wife?"

"Yes, because it will take me the rest of my life to unravel them all. And with each layer I discover, I fall deeper in love. Tyler is the most complex woman I've ever met. She seems fragile, but Tyler is a fighter and a survivor."

"I'm a fighter too."

"No doubt, but you fight for all the wrong reasons—hey, you said you wanted the truth. This is one conversation I never thought we would have, especially not with you in your underwear."

"Funny, Andre. I feel like a fool prancing down here in my lingerie thinking I would seduce you back into my bed, all while you're still in love with Tyler Blake. How in the hell did I miss that one?"

"If it makes you feel any better, you still got it."

"You mean that?"

"Definitely, but Chantal, get your mind right. Because all of that beauty isn't going to teach our daughter how to grow up to be a real woman. And on that note, I'm out."

Chantal followed Andre to the door, "Goodbye," she said, giving him a hug and kiss. Chantal knew that Andre would always be an excellent father to Melanie, but it was time for her to finally close the chapter to that part of her life.

"You have to get over this need to protect Tyler. You're not her father and you're no longer her lover," Maria pointed out as she laid on the bed watching William pack for his trip to New York.

"Must we keep discussing this?"

"When you stop trying to keep such a tight leash on Tyler, then of course we can. It would bring me nothing but pleasure to stop making my daughter a topic of our daily chats."

"Then stop."

"How can I when you constantly baby her?"

"I don't baby Tyler. But she is very dear to me and always will be. If you can't accept that, I don't see how..." William's voice trailed off, not wanting to leave for his trip on the outs with Maria. He was actually very fond of her and enjoyed the time they shared. But her constant nagging about Tyler was a sore spot for him. He cared deeply for Tyler and always would, but he had longed accepted that their love affair was over and would never be again. But the need to protect her remained intact.

"See how what, William?"

"It was nothing."

"Oh it was something. But so we're clear, I won't be competing for your affection against my daughter."

"I'm not asking you to."

"Your actions are showing otherwise. I suggest you use this trip to decide what direction you want this relationship to go. I never believed in playing second fiddle and I'm not about to start now."

"Are you giving me an ultimatum, Maria?"

"Well, now that you've brought it up, I would say that I am." Those were Maria's parting words before entering the bathroom and slamming the door behind her.

Tyler double-checked that she had everything she needed for the trip before heading to the airport. "Deanna, are you ready? We're already running late."

"Yes, Ms. Blake. I was making sure I had all my belongings in order."

"I'm thrilled you're accompanying me on this trip. That way even when I'm working I can have Christian nearby, especially since we're running behind on filming and I know William is going to work the hell out of me."

"Whatever I can do to help, Ms. Blake. I know how stressful your life is, being a movie star and all."

"You have no idea. It's one headache after another. I've been in such a slump, but seeing Christian will be an incredible boost. I hope you enjoy yourself too. You haven't been yourself these last couple of weeks."

"I'm fine. I'm just getting up there in age and my bones don't work like they used too."

"Oh please, you're only sixty and you look gorgeous." Tyler was only somewhat lying. It was apparent that Deanna had been a beautiful woman at one time in her life, but that beauty had long faded. Her stunning mahogany complexion and delicate features were graced with premature wrinkles and heavy eyes that showed signs of a life full of stress.

"Thank you, Ms. Blake, that's truly a compliment coming from a woman as beautiful as you."

"It's the truth. Now let's get out of here. We have a private jet to catch."

Chapter Fifteen

Feel Like Fire

When Tyler arrived in New York, the first thing she did was go pick Christian up from Brian's home in Alpine, New Jersey. It was as if Christian could feel his mother's presence, because even before the Limo pulled up to the winding driveway, he came running out the Palm Beach style façade, done in concrete stucco. Tyler didn't wait for the driver to open her door. She jumped out, ran to her son and grabbed him. "Oh, Christian, I've missed you so much," she said, squeezing him tightly.

"Mommy, I missed you too." Christian's little arms and hands wrapped around Tyler's neck was the best warmth of love she had ever felt.

Tyler noticed Brian walking out carrying a couple of bags. "I packed some of his clothes and favorite toys."

"Thank you for taking such wonderful care of Christian while I was in the hospital and working. But I'm thrilled he's going to come back home with me."

"I'm happy to be going home with you too, Mommy," he said, holding on tightly to his mother.

"I'm going to miss you, little man." Brian nuzzled the top of Christian's head.

"I'll see you again real soon, Daddy."

"You promise?"

"Promise." They gave each other a high five.

"I'll call you," Tyler said, feeling lightened that her encounter with Brian went with such ease.

When they got back in the Limo Tyler introduced Christian to Deanna. "Baby, Deanna lives with me in Malibu. While I'm working she'll watch over you and make sure that you're having fun."

"Hi there. Aren't you a handsome little boy," Deanna said, reaching over to pat Christian's hand, but he moved it away.

"You don't have to be scared, honey. Deanna is a friend of Mommy's."

"How about later on I take you out for ice cream?" Deanna suggested.

"Okay, ice cream sounds good," Christian cheered.

Tyler turned and smiled at Deanna, happy she was able to break the ice with her son.

Shari and Chantal parked in front of Charlie Trotter's which was discreetly located in Chicago's Lincoln Park area. Shari handed her keys to the valet and then they made their way to the entrance.

Upon walking through the front door they were greeted with the aromatic sweetness of magnificent floral and fruit arrangements. The ladies followed the host as they passed the two-story bar before being seated in one of the unique dining rooms, all of which was presented in an elegant, quiet style. The host knew to seat Chantal and Shari in the South dining room, which was designated to accommodate smaller parties. Due to the obscene conversations they engaged in, privacy was always of importance.

"Girl, tell me what the hell is going on. You've been here for damn near a week and this is our first time hooking up, and I know it got something to do with that damn Andre," Shari said, sipping a glass of Santiago Ruiz wine.

"Bitch, you know it do," Chantal admitted.

"Do not tell me you lured that man back in your bed."

"I ain't going to lie, I tried, and tried hard. I put on my fiercest bra and panty set with the hooker shoes to match. Girl, I was smelling all good. If I wasn't me, I would want to fuck myself."

"I know that's right," Shari said, smacking Chantal's hand.

"But Andre was not having it. His nose is wide open for Tyler. Girl, he is really in love."

"He told you that?"

"Yep, and you know what? I'm actually happy for him."

"What?" Shari asked, surprised.

"You ain't the only one surprised. I was shocked that I took it so well. But after I played myself trying to seduce his ass, we really sat down and he kept it real with me. There was no bullshit excuses or games being played, he was being sincere. How can I not respect that?"

"True, but it still must hurt. You've known Andre for a real long time and the two of you have Melanie."

"And maybe that's what makes it easier to let go. Melanie loves Andre so much, and I don't want him not having that relationship with her that she deserves because the crazy baby mama trying to tempt him into bed every time he comes over to visit. My daughter don't deserve that shit. It's time for me to let go and get my own life, and let the relationship I have with Andre be just about our daughter."

"Bitch, who the hell is you and what happened to my friend, Chantal?"

"Stop playing."

"You need to stop playing like all of a sudden you 'un got some good sense."

Chantal couldn't help but laugh at Shari's comment. "I have acted like a fool when it came to that man. Girl, you know when I got in that fight with Tyler at the charity event we both fell in the pool. So I asked Andre why he loved Tyler so much. He said one of the reasons was because she was a fighter, so I told him I was a fighter too. Shit! He said yeah, but you always fighting for the wrong reasons—if that ain't nothing but the truth. So, child, when they say the truth will set you free, I needed to hear that."

"Are you saying you're turning over a new leaf?"

"What's that saying... a leopard can't ever change its spots? I'm still the same Chantal, but after that talk I had with Andre I've just wised up a bit. I've finally accepted that Andre Jackson doesn't want to be with me, let alone marry me, and never did. He's in love with Tyler and I wish them nothing but misery." Both ladies burst out laughing and Chantal clapped her hands. "But seriously, I wish them the best, but instead of wasting all my energy on them I need to find a man who is perfect for me."

"And that would be…"

"Someone who accepts all my flaws and appreciates me more because of them."

"I don't know anybody that crazy."

"I do."

T-Roc mentally prepared himself for a second day of grueling work. They were behind on filming and William was anxious to wrap up the movie, and so was he.

He enjoyed the time he was able to spend with Tyler, but his entire life was on hold during filming and T-Roc wasn't use to those sorts of restraints. He was also becoming frustrated because with all the schemes he pulled, he didn't seem any closer to making Tyler his. He underestimated Tyler's love for Andre because even though he pushed her away, Tyler remained committed to him. "But maybe all hope isn't lost," T-Roc said as he passed the gift store on his way out the Essex House Hotel lobby.

Tyler kissed a still sleeping Christian on his forehead before leaving out. She closed the door and saw Deanna coming out of one of the other bedrooms in the penthouse suite. "Good morning, Deanna, I hope you slept well."

"I did, but I still can't get over how big this hotel room is. It's like a house."

"Yes, but we need it with all three of us staying here. It's not home, but close enough to it."

"Being a Hollywood actress sure does come with a lot of perks. It must be like living a fairytale."

"It can feel that way sometimes, but I know you've heard of that saying, everything that glitters isn't gold. It's nothing but the truth. For every wonderful thing that happens in my career, it seems my personal life takes all the punches. But enough of me feeling sorry for myself. I can't be late or William will have a hernia." Tyler grabbed her purse to head out. "I left money on the table for you and Christian's activities for the day, but make sure you bring him to the set for lunch."

"I will, Ms. Blake. See you later on."

On her way to the elevator, Tyler turned her cell back on after cutting it off before going to sleep last night, not wanting to be disturbed since she had been exhausted. In less than two seconds it started going off and she wondered who was calling so early. "Hello."

"Hi, Tyler, it's me Ian."

"Hi. You got my message I left last night?"

"Yeah, but my battery was dead and I just checked them. It's too bad you and your son can't come to the game. I was looking forward to seeing you and meeting him."

"I know, but we're working our asses off finishing this movie and I won't have the time."

"What time are you going to be done?"

"Probably around ten or eleven."

"Can you squeeze me in for a drink?"

Tyler hesitated before answering. "I guess one drink wouldn't hurt."

"Wonderful. Where are you staying?"

"The Essex House."

"Over there on Central Park South?"

"Yep, that's it."

"How about we meet at Journeys Lounge? It's right inside your hotel."

"Perfect."

"Okay, so I'll call you when I'm on my way."

When Tyler hung up with Ian, she checked her voicemail hoping Andre had called, but in her gut knowing he hadn't. The distance between her and Andre was breaking Tyler's heart. That feeling of abandonment was ripping through her soul and brought back memories of when she was a little girl waving good-bye to her daddy from the backseat as he chased after her mother's car, sobbing and begging for them to come back. But they never went back, and Tyler's father never came back looking for them—or so she thought.

T-Roc was on set ready to work when Tyler arrived. He waited patiently while she was getting done in hair and makeup. He welcomed the extra time to plan how he would make his move.

"Let's go everybody," William yelled, interrupting T-Roc's scheming. "Where's Tyler?"

"Still in hair and makeup," T-Roc answered.

"Not anymore. Sorry about the hold up," Tyler said, stepping out the trailer.

"Come on people, let's go. Time is money," William declared.

T-Roc realized now wasn't the time to make his move. They spent the rest of the morning and early part of the afternoon shooting in front of Radio City Music Hall on Sixth Avenue and 51st Street.

At around two o'clock William finally screamed, "Cut." to everyone's relief.

"Tyler, can I talk to you for a second?" T-Roc asked before she headed towards her trailer.

"Can it wait? Deanna just brought Christian for lunch and we only have an hour."

"Sure." T-Roc went back into his trailer and kept checking until he saw Deanna and Christian leave. They stayed longer than an hour, and T-Roc knew he had a small window of time to talk to Tyler before William made everyone get back to work. He hurried to Tyler's trailer and knocked on the door.

"Who is it?"

"T-Roc."

"Hi. Is William ready for us?" Tyler asked, letting T-Roc inside.

"Not yet, but I needed to speak with you anyway."

"I forgot about that. What did you want to tell me?" Tyler sat down in front of the mirror touching up her makeup.

"I think there is something you should see before you're bombarded by the paparazzi."

Tyler turned around and saw the magazine T-Roc was holding. She grabbed it out of his hand. On the front cover of the US Weekly was a small snapshot of Andre in front of a house, kissing a woman clad in her lingerie who appeared to be Chantal. The caption above read, *'Andre Jackson caught in the arms of another woman.'*

When Tyler turned to read the inside story, it read, *"While Tyler Blake is away, Andre Jackson seeks comfort in the arms of the mother of his child, Chantal Morgan"*.

It had another picture with the two of them hugging, and then Andre getting in his car to leave. The article went on the give an overview of Chantal and Andre's relationship up to the point where he left her at the altar, and then Chantal hitting Tyler with her car. It even insinuated that Andre was the one that made sure Chantal never went to jail for the crime. They also quoted an inside source speaking about the recent fight the women had at the charity event where Chantal ended up being dragged out in handcuffs. The story was salacious at the very least, and a tremendous blow to Tyler.

"Tyler, are you okay?"

Tyler rested her elbows on the console table, then put her head down in the palm of her hands. Before she answered T-Roc's question, she heard the chime of her cell. She picked it up and saw Andre's number. "Now Andre decides to call after his face is splashed across Us Weekly," Tyler said, tossing her phone back down. "Well it's too late. I don't want to hear it."

"I didn't want to be the one to show you this, but I thought you deserved to know."

"Of course. Better I hear it from you then the other millions of people who would love to tell me. When I was a little girl dreaming of being a movie star, never did I believe it came with having your heart crushed in front of the entire world. I wish someone had forewarned me how high the price of fame is."

T-Roc watched as Tyler picked her purse up and took out one of the pills he had given her. She grabbed her bottled water and swallowed it down and said, "Time to get back to work."

"Tyler, pick up the damn phone," Andre screamed in the receiver and then slammed it down on the table in his hotel room when the call went to voice mail for the tenth time. *I can't believe this shit. I go to Chicago to get away from the media, but they still manage to find me and put this bullshit on the front of a magazine. I know Tyler believes this garbage, and I can't even blame her because if I was her I would too. Damn, if she would only let me explain.* Andre broke out of his thoughts when he heard his cell ringing and prayed it was Tyler. "Hello, Tyler," he answered, not bothering to see what number came up.

"Sorry, it's me Chantal."

"Hi, Chantal," he said with disappointment in his voice.

"I guess you already seen the magazine. My phone been ringing off the hook."

"Hell yeah, I can't believe this shit," Andre blasted back.

"For the record I had no idea there was a photographer lurking in the bushes waiting to snap a picture of us."

"Them motherfuckers been on me ever since me and Tyler became a couple, it's not your fault. I should've been more careful."

"But you didn't do anything wrong. You have to explain to Tyler that the picture is deceiving. If you want I'll call her myself."

"Don't. I appreciate the gesture but trust me you calling Tyler won't make the situation any better."

"Well have you spoken to her?"

"She won't speak to me. I keep calling her but she doesn't pick up. I've really fucked up. With everything else going on this is the last thing we need. I don't know how many more test our relationship can endure."

"Damn, Andre this is fucked up. If it helps the press has been blowing up my phone asking for a comment and I keep telling them that nothing happened. You were only over visiting your daughter."

"I'm sure it's a little hard for them to believe with the attire you were wearing."

"I already felt bad, now you making me feel even more guilty."

"That's not my intention. I have to figure out how to make this right. I gotta go, Chantal. I'll talk to you later," Andre said hanging up. He walked over and opened the Tiffany & Co. box and admired the X line platinum bracelet with clip from the Victoria collection he had planned to surprise Tyler with when he begged her forgiveness for shutting her out. He imagined how the forty round brilliant diamonds and four marquise diamonds would sparkle on Tyler's wrist. But with this latest fiasco Andre wasn't sure if he would ever have the chance to see.

When Tyler got back to her hotel room, Christian was already sound asleep. She stepped in the marble floored bathroom and turned on the shower. The hot water engulfing her body was exactly what she needed. As she lathered every curve, she replayed the tons of messages Andre left on her phone. He vehemently denied the article being true. Tyler's heart wanted to believe him but her head was screaming something else. But tonight, Tyler wanted to forget the turmoil her relationship with Andre was in.

After her long shower, Tyler slipped on a satin, light steel blue, billowy sleeved cocktail dress perfectly balanced with a plunging neckline that gave the style a carefree quality. She lifted her loose curls up, leaving a few to frame her face. She dabbed on some Mac Foolishly Fab Plush lip glass, grabbed her peach Bottega Venetta clutch and headed out to meet Ian.

When Tyler entered the Journeys Lounge it had a tranquil vibe. The décor was a transcontinental travel of the 1930's theme. She noticed Ian sitting in a booth by the wood-burning fireplace, which complimented the clubby ambiance of mahogany paneled walls and Persian carpets. "Sorry I'm so late," she said, sitting down.

"I'm happy you showed up."

"Why wouldn't I?"

"Work, and I know you have a lot on your mind."

"Let me guess. You either saw or heard about the article on Andre and Chantal."

"I wasn't going to bring it up, but yeah, I did."

"Does that mean you're no longer seeing Chantal?"

"That's been over. I wouldn't say it ever started. What about you and Andre?"

"I don't know. I haven't spoken to him, but from the messages he left me he claims the story isn't true."

"Do you believe him?"

"I want to, but Chantal dressed in her underwear, him kissing her, a picture is worth a thousand words. But you know what, I promised myself that for this one night I wouldn't let my mind be consumed with Andre."

"Say no more. We can talk about how beautiful you look in that dress."

"Cute. So who won the game?"

"You know we killed those whack ass Knicks. Them clowns can't win any games. I wish you could've been there."

"Me too. I think Christian would've enjoyed it."

"How old is your son?"

"Five. What about your little one?"

"She's three."

"I bet she's adorable."

"Yeah, she is. Every time I look at her I think about the child we could've had together. I'll never forgive myself for throwing you down those stairs."

"Don't do this, Ian."

"I can't help but think that if it never happened we would still be together."

"I've learned that you can't dwell on the what ifs. I mean, what if I never slept with T-Roc? Then you would've never thrown me down the stairs and the whole chain of events would be different. But I did sleep with him and you did react the way that you did, and we both should take it as a learning experience."

"One to grow on."

"Exactly."

"I hear you. The thing is, with all the time that has passed I'm still not over you."

Ian rubbed Tyler's arm and his touch was enticing. She longed to be held by Andre, but wondered if being with Ian would be a wonderful alternative. He did know her body and the one area they never had a problem with was the bedroom.

"Tyler, we're more mature now. I believe we can make it work this time."

"Isn't this cozy, my cousin and my favorite girl," T-Roc said, positioned in an imposing manner.

"T-Roc, what are you doing here?" Tyler asked, startled.

"The question is, why are you with *him*?"

"Who the fuck is you to be questioning her?" Ian popped, standing up.

"You can't be running back into this cat's arms after he threw you down the stairs and killed our baby." T-Roc moved in closer.

"Motherfucker, that was *my* seed she was carrying," Ian spit.

"Would you two stop? Honestly, we don't know whose baby it was, and at this point does it even matter."

"Hell yeah it matters, because he's responsible for taking out my unborn child," T-Roc pointed his finger at Ian. "The only reason I didn't have your ass put six feet under is because we blood. But I'll be damn if I'm about to stand here and watch you break bread with this dude."

"Then leave," Tyler yelled. "You act like you own me, but you don't and never have."

"I've destroyed lives for you. You owe me." T-Roc's stare felt like an electric shock through her veins. His words were reflexive and she didn't know how to respond.

T-Roc then grabbed Tyler's arm and held it firmly. "You need to stop fighting it and realize you belong to me."

"You're crazy."

"Get your fucking hands off of her," Ian barked

"You stay out of this," T-Roc said, using his other hand to shove Ian's shoulder, and that's when all hell broke loose.

Ian swung on T-Roc and his jaw rocked to the side from the impact of the punch. T-Roc quickly gained his composure and reached over Tyler, clenching Ian's neck. The open bottle of champagne Ian had on the table flew in Tyler's direction and drenched her dress. She moved from being in the center of their brawl as they continued to exchange blows. They were now falling over the table and about to hit the floor until a few husky hotel security men came over and broke the fight up.

"I'm not done with you. I'm going to fuck you up," T-Roc threatened, huffing rapidly.

"Bring it on," Ian shot back.

"Both of you are out of here," one of the security men groaned as they led T-Roc and Ian out of the lounge.

The live piano music once again filled the air, and Tyler sat down wondering if and when the theatrics would ever end.

Chapter Sixteen

Angel in Disguise

"Ella, you look amazing," Tyler gushed as she and her sister sat in a back table at the Cuban restaurant, Café Fuego for lunch.

"Thank you, lil sis."

"And your hair—this short shag with the blond highlights is fabulous. You definitely have the whole fashion designer image on lock. I hope you brought some outfits for me."

"You know I did. The host has them hanging in a garment bag up front. So you better rock them clothes on the red carpet and give me a shout-out."

"That goes without saying. I can't wait to show off my sister's clothes. I'm so proud of you."

"And me of you. You're famous. Those same tabloids we would read as teenagers, now your face is all over them. Talk about surreal. I have to remind myself that you're my sister. How does it feel to walk outside and everyone knows your name?"

"Some days on top of the world, but on most, weighed down. But the weird thing is when I'm with Christian it puts things in perspective because to him I'm just 'Mom'."

"That's beautiful. Where is my nephew anyway?"

"With Deanna, the maid-slash-nanny. She's been incredible with Christian. At first I wasn't sure if he would feel comfortable with her but now he adores her, which is awesome, especially since he's coming back to Malibu with me."

"That's wonderful. I know Christian must be so happy."

"He is and I'm ecstatic. Brian was wonderful with him, but it's time for him to come home and be with his Mommy."

"How is Brian?"

"Better. He doesn't seem to hate me anymore. And if he does he's learned how to hide it," Tyler smiled.

"After that awful custody battle I didn't know if you all would ever get to a place that you could be civil with each other.

It's good to hear you all are making progress, especially for Christian's sake."

"I know."

"And how's Mother? Did she drive you crazy during her visit?"

"I guess you haven't spoken to her recently, because before I left, mother was still in LA."

"Really? She must have met a man."

"Damn sure did, and not just any man. William Donovan."

"Your ex-lover and the director of your movie?"

"One and the same."

"Mother never ceases to amaze me," Ella said, shaking her head. "How in the hell did that happen.

"I made the dumb mistake of bringing her to the movie set. She got one whiff of William and it was all she wrote."

"Did you tell her you all had been seriously involved at one time?"

"Of course, but she blamed our relationship on my daddy issues, which I won't deny that I have, but still I used to have sex with William. Are there *any* boundaries?"

"The mold was certainly broken when Mother was created. She can find an excuse for every deplorable act she commits."

"You ain't never lied about that."

"Enough of her. How much longer are you going to be in town?"

"Today we finished filming, thank goodness, so we're out of here tomorrow. I've been in this city for too long. I'm ready to go home."

"Who was your co-star in the movie again?"

"T-Roc."

"How could I forget that? How did it go?"

"He's an excellent actor and I think the movie will be amazing, but T-Roc the person is an absolute nightmare. The last few days of shooting were draining. He got in a huge fight with Ian a few days ago and I didn't want to be around him. But of course work is work, and no matter how much you detest your leading man, I had a job to do."

"Why did he and Ian get in a fight?"

"Still living in the past, that's why."

"That's a shame. Do they really need to be fighting over an engaged woman?"

Tyler looked down at the pink diamond ring on her finger. Even with the chaos in her relationship with Andre she hadn't taken off his ring.

"Is everything okay between you and Andre?"

"You haven't read the stories?"

"Of course I have, but with you being my sister I've learned that everything you read isn't true."

"I wish that was the case, but I don't even know what the truth is. We are having serious problems and I have no idea if we'll get through this."

"Have you discussed your reservations with Andre?"

"When I was desperate to speak to him he had no words for me, and now that he's dying to plead his case to me, I have no words for him."

"If you love him as much as you've told me, then find the words. Real love is too precious to give up on."

"Thanks, Ella, I needed to hear that. I feel a little better."

"I hope my surprise will make you feel even better."

"What surprise?"

"Brace yourself. You'll be taken aback at first, but this is the beginning to all your healing."

"Ella, you're totally confusing me."

"I want you to turn around slowly and say hello to…"

Anticipation wouldn't allow Tyler to wait. She had already turned around before Ella could finish her sentence.

"D-d-daddy," Tyler stuttered as if seeing a ghost. It had been over twenty years since the last time Tyler had seen her father, but the eyes never lie, and looking into his was like staring back into her own.

Tyler stood up from her chair, walked closer and reached out her arm gently touching his face. She wanted to feel the softness of his skin and the outline of each feature from his nose, eyes and high cheekbones. She rubbed her fingers through the low curls in his hair and finally hugged him to take in the smell of his skin that she had been deprived of for so long. "Daddy, I missed you." When she released the words from her mouth, the flow of tears followed.

"My sweet angel, Daddy missed you too."

"You guys come sit down."

"I've dreamed about sitting down with both my daughters for so long. Dreams really do come true."

"Daddy, I have so many questions."

"So did I when we first spoke. Initially when he called I didn't believe it was really Daddy, but within a few minutes I knew."

"Ella, how long ago was that?"

"About a month. I knew you were coming to New York and we both felt it would be better if you reunited in person."

"Daddy, where have you been?"

"I've been living in North Carolina for some years now. But a day never went by that I didn't miss my girls."

"Why didn't you come back for us, Daddy?" Tyler couldn't ask the question without breaking down and crying.

"Oh, dear God, I always prayed that before He took me out this world that I would have the chance to tell you that I did come back." Tyler's father opened his bag, and there were tons of unopened letters stamped as 'undeliverable' were inside, and he dropped some on the table. "They were all sent back to me. Your mother got so fed up with me trying to make contact that she came to see me with her new husband. Maria said she had married a rich, successful man and you girls had a new father that you adored and you hated me for putting my hands on her and never wanted to see me again. I was riddled with shame for you girls witnessing me hurting your mother and couldn't blame you. I didn't feel worthy to have you in my life, so I did what Maria asked and left all of you alone. It was too painful knowing you were living in the same state and not be able to see you so I moved away. Every once in a while I would call to see how you both were doing and Maria would say I was dead to you, and that if I kept on calling she would have me taken care of permanently. I know I should've fought harder to see you but I believed I had nothing to offer and you were happier and better off without me. Please forgive me."

"Growing up I always felt something must be wrong with me if my own father didn't want me. I would go from one horrible relationship to another believing that I was never worthy of real love from a man because the man I needed the most had turned his back on me, which was you. But now I know that you did come back for me, and that makes all the difference in the world." Tears fell from both Ella and their dad at hearing Tyler's painful confession.

They all held each other tightly, and Tyler knew that Ella was right; this was the beginning of her healing.

"I can't believe your ass is going back to LA already. I thought you would at least stay put for a month," Shari said, driving Chantal to the airport.

"I have some unfinished business to handle there."

"Unfinished business like what?"

"When it's finished I'll let you know."

"Alright, smartass. We been like this," Shari crossed two fingers on her right hand, "Since we were damn near in Pampers, and now you want to hold out on me."

"It ain't like that. I'm about to tread in unfamiliar territory and I'm afraid if I discuss it out loud I might change my mind."

"Boy oh boy, I can't wait to hear how this plays out."

"If you keep running your mouth, it might not."

"Next subject. So how is Andre holding up after he got caught out there?"

"I told you that didn't nothing happen between me Andre."

"I know, but that picture didn't relay the same message. Has Tyler forgiven his black ass yet?"

"We spoke briefly when he came to my parents' house to say bye to Melanie before he went back to LA."

"Your parents' house?"

"Oh yeah, after that story hit he said he wasn't coming back to my crib. He would see Melanie at my parents'.."

"Tyler got that dude shook."

"Damn sure do. She still not answering his calls."

"Wow, Tyler gangsta with hers. Andre finally met his match. Someone who can put him on pause longer than he can them."

"I can't front. I knew the broad had balls when after I slapped her she came back with that right hook. I didn't think she had it in her."

"I would've paid money to see the two of you go at it that night. Sound like Tyler got the best of you."

"We got the best of each other."

"Un hum, if you say so."

"Whatever. I ain't fucking with you. Like I said, I have some business to handle and a flight to catch."

"Then get the fuck out the car," Shari said jokingly, stopping in front of the American Airlines terminal.

"I'll call and let you know what the hell is going on."

"Do that, because I never know with your crazy ass."

"Bye, girl."

As Chantal waited to have her luggage checked, in she was having second thoughts about the decision she made, but decided to move forward. She was a lot of things, but a coward wasn't one of them.

Tyler arrived back to her hotel suite feeling like a brand new woman with a newfound confidence. "Hi, Deanna. Where's Christian? I have exciting news for him. I want to take him to meet his grandpa."

Deanna was bringing her luggage to the sitting area when Tyler walked in and she didn't respond to Tyler's question. "Deanna, you don't have to bring your luggage out, we're not leaving until tomorrow afternoon. Where's Christian? Is he in the room taking a nap?"

"Christian is fine."

"Where is he? I saw my dad today for the first time in over twenty years and I want to take Christian to meet him. Isn't it wonderful?"

"It hasn't been that long since you've seen Michael."

"Michael. Michael is my stepfather's name. How did you even know that?"

"I know a lot more about you than you think, Tyler. So now that your biological father is back, you just disregard Michael after you and your mother stole him and turned him against his real family."

"What are you talking about, and where is my son?" An avalanche of worry fell on Tyler. She ran to all the bedrooms, opened the doors, and there was no sign of Christian. She then searched both bathrooms and the closet. All of Christian's clothes and other belongs were gone. "Deanna, where is my son?" Tyler screamed.

"He is somewhere safe waiting for me to return so we can leave."

"Leave. You think you're leaving with my son? I'm calling the police."

"Put that phone down right now."

Tyler dropped the receiver when Deanna brandished a gun. "What is going on? Are you trying to kidnap my son for a ransom? Tell me how much. I'll give you any amount that you want, just give me back my son."

"I'll tell you what. If you bring back *my* son then I'll give you back *yours*. But then that would be impossible even for a glamorous, rich movie star like you since my son is dead."

"Who is your son and what does it have to do with me?"

"It has everything to do with you. You stole my son's father, and because of your lies, Evan never had the life he was entitled to."

"No, no you can't be Evan's mother. Your name is Deanna Cooper."

"Evan had his father's last name. Michael never married me. I wasn't good enough. Instead he chose to marry your slutty mother and be a father to kids that weren't even his. He turned his back on his own blood because of your lies. My son had his whole future ahead of him, and with your one accusation it was all ruined."

"It wasn't an accusation. Your son tried to rape me and when I was only six years old. I didn't have to lie about any of it. His father caught him and saw it with his own eyes."

"You're a liar! You're a filthy whore like your mother and seduced my son."

"I was six years old. Do you know how sick you sound?"

"Shut up! Your lies drove my son to kill himself and now it's time for you to rot in hell."

"Deanna, don't do this. Christian needs me."

"He'll have me. I'll take care of him. By the time they find your dead body we will be long gone. It's only fair; one son for another."

Both women turned to look at the door as they heard someone knocking. "Don't say a word," Deanna mouthed with her finger firmly gripped on the trigger. The knocking continued.

"Tyler, are you there?" Tyler recognized T-Roc's voice and wanted to scream for help but was afraid Deanna would shoot to kill. Deanna was only a few feet away from her, and all Tyler could think about was never seeing Christian again.

There was a long silence and both women thought T-Roc gave up, and then unexpectedly the knocking started back up, startling Deanna.

Tyler used the distraction to her advantage. She quickly grabbed a piece of luggage that Deanna had brought out and tossed it at her. One shot went off as the gun flew out of Deanna's hand.

"Tyler, what's going on in there?" T-Roc yelled as he tried to kick the door down

"T-Roc, call the police," Tyler screamed as she dove to the floor trying to reach the gun before Deanna. Tyler didn't know if it was pure determination, anger, strength or a combination of all three, but Deanna was much stronger than Tyler thought and was putting up a hell of a fight as the women struggled to gain control of the gun. Tyler pounded her elbow into Deanna's stomach.

"Ouch," Deanna cried out.

Tyler reached out and grabbed the gun and the tables had now turned. She ran to the door and let T-Roc in.

"I've never been so happy to see you in all my life," Tyler said.

"What happened?" T-Roc asked, seeing Deanna trying to get up holding her stomach.

"This psycho took my son and tried to kill me."

"What in the hell, are you serious?"

"Dead serious. Did you call the police?"

"No, I was too busy trying to kick the door down."

"Keep your eye on her. Make sure she doesn't move," Tyler said, walking over to the phone and dialing 911."

When Tyler came back in the room she heard Deanna say to T-Roc, "You better let me go or I'll tell Tyler everything."

"Everything like what?"

"I don't know what this crazy woman is talking about," T-Roc said.

Tyler stared back at Deanna.

"You thought when my son killed himself your secrets died with him."

"Who is your son?"

"Evan McNeil, or that would be Gee to you. I knew all about your arrangement with him. Who do you think he trusted with all the money you gave him to handle your dirty work?"

"Tyler, she's delusional."

"No I'm not. T-Roc hired my son to make your life miserable. From having William Donovan catch you in the bed with Andre Jackson so he could replace him in the role of 'Angel', to having that story leaked about Andre in the Los Angeles Times.

He was behind it all. He was even sleeping with your best friend, Chrissie to pump information from her. He orchestrated everything, and everyone else was his puppets."

T-Roc jumped forward to get the gun out of Tyler's hand. "Shoot this lying, bitch. She's crazy."

Tyler moved her hand out of T-Roc's reach. "Get away from me."

"Tyler, you can't believe this preposterous nonsense."

"The pieces to the puzzle are falling into place, one misfortune after another, never understanding the reason why."

"Because I love you."

"Stop using that word to describe what you feel for me because it isn't love. I don't know what to call such twisted and demented behavior."

"Ms. put your weapon down," the police ordered after finally showing up and interrupting the grilling she was about to put on T-Roc.

Tyler placed the gun on the floor and the officer came over and picked it up. "Was it you that call us?" he directed his question to Tyler.

"Yes, my name is Tyler Blake, and this woman took my son and tried to kill me."

"What is your name?"

Deanna remained silent

"Her name is Deanna Cooper," Tyler informed the officer.

"Deanna Cooper, you're under arrest. You have the right to remain silent. Anything you say or do can be used against you in a court of law…" As the officer continued to read Deanna her rights, once he finished he began drilling her about Christian's whereabouts. But she said nothing.

Another plainclothes officer sat down and spoke to Tyler. "Ms. Blake, we will find your son. An Amber Alert has been issued. Please give us as many details as possible—what he was wearing, any distinctive features or marks."

Tyler answered every question and sat patiently waiting for any news on her son's wellbeing.

"Tyler, they'll find Christian, and I don't believe he's been harmed," T-Roc said, sitting down beside Tyler.

"T-Roc, I don't even want to hear the sound of your voice right now."

"Please don't be angry with me. I did a terrible thing by hiring someone to break up you and Andre, but never did I know Evan was your stepbrother. I was in shock when Deanna revealed that."

"That's the only thing you're guilty of is sabotaging my relationship with Andre?"

"Yes, and perhaps manipulating situations to secure the role in this movie, but frankly, I believe that was justified."

"Why aren't I surprised?"

"Because you know that the role of Damien should have gone to me. Instead you gave it to Andre for your own selfish reasons."

"You hire a maniac to ruin my life, have sex with my best friend to obtain information to use against me, but I'm selfish? My gut tells me you're responsible for a lot more, and if I can ever prove it you'll be walking out in handcuffs, just like Deanna."

Before T-Roc could counter, the detective walked up. "We have good news, Ms. Blake. Your son has been located and he appears to be unharmed."

"What, where is he?" Tyler jumped up relieved and astonished Christian had been located so soon.

"The officers are bringing him up as we speak. He was actually down the street in a parking garage in the car Deanna Cooper rented. Apparently he's been sitting there alone for some time now. A pedestrian became suspicious and contacted the authorities."

"Praise the Lord."

"I told you he would be fine," T-Roc said, rubbing Tyler's back.

Tyler flexed her body forward not wanting to feel T-Roc's touch.

Three officers came through the door, and at first Tyler didn't see Christian because he was being blocked, but when he heard Tyler call out his name he yelled out, "Mommy, Mommy," breaking free from the grasp of one of the officer's.

"Oh, baby, I'm so happy you're okay. Mommy will never let you go again." Tyler held her son tightly, knowing he was truly the most important thing in her life.

Chapter Seventeen

Share My World

After the terrifying ordeal with Deanna in New York, Tyler became increasingly cautious about the people she had around her and her son. Once back in Malibu, she used a reputable firm that William recommended to do a meticulous check on her security and to hire additional help. Tyler then began the task of hiring a full time nanny for Christian. That required a grueling interview process. When the nanny agency selected their top picks, the next round of screening went through the security firm. The final step was for Tyler to meet them. She always had Christian sit with her during each interview because Tyler couldn't forget that the very first time he met Deanna, he pulled away from her. Tyler took that as a sign that a child's initial reaction could be the most important.

As Tyler waited for a potential nanny to arrive for her first interview of the morning, her cell rang. "Hello," she answered.

"I've left you several messages. Why haven't you called me back?"

"I'm sorry, Ian, so much has been going on and I haven't had time."

"How's your son?"

"Wonderful, and thank you for all the gifts you sent him. He especially loved the signed basketball and jersey. Christian wanted to thank you personally. He couldn't believe that his mother was friends with basketball great, Ian Addison."

"Yeah, although I was hoping we could be more than friends."

"Ian…"

"You don't have to answer that now," Ian said, cutting Tyler off. "But last time we saw each other I felt we still had a deep connection and maybe there was a chance for us. If T-Roc hadn't shown up, who knows what could've happened that night between us."

"You're right, but maybe it's good that he did show up. I mean I wish the fight never broke out between you guys. But I think I was vulnerable that evening and things could've gone too far and I would've woken up the next morning with a lot of regrets."

"How could you regret letting me make love to you?"

"Because I'm still in love with Andre, and until I've come to a resolution, my heart or my mind aren't ready to be with anyone else. I don't want to sleep with one man to get over another one anymore. I rather embrace the pain and disappointment, heal from it, and then move on."

"Wow, you really have grown up. You're not the Tyler Blake I used to know, but I still love you just the same. If and when you decide to give us another chance, you know how to reach me. I'll always be here for you."

"Thank you, Ian. Bye."

Tyler hung up the phone and looked around, staring at the pink and red rose compositions, vandella roses, pink peony, and white hydrangeas. Her living room resembled a flower shop, all courtesy of Andre. She then stared at her wrist, admiring the gorgeous Tiffany diamond bracelet that was lying on the center of the bed when she came back from her trip to New York. The card read, *I still love you, Love Andre*. But Tyler couldn't bring herself to call him. The picture of him and Chantal remained fresh in her mind, and with all Andre's denials, not knowing for sure was eating her up.

"Ms. Blake?" The sound of one of Tyler's security guards snapped her out of deep thought. "The guard at the gate informed me the nanny is here for the interview, and also that a woman trying to trespass was apprehended."

"What woman?"

"He's bringing her up now."

Tyler followed the security man to the front door. The nanny came in first, and right behind her was Chantal being held tightly by a guard.

"You're hurting my arms. Can you please let go?" Chantal shrieked through clenched teeth.

"Ms. Blake, this woman claims she is a friend of yours."

"I didn't say friend, I said we know each other. There is a difference."

"Call the police. This woman is trespassing and in violation of the restraining order. Again, sorry about that," Tyler said, turning to the nanny. "You can follow me inside."

"Tyler, wait. I must speak to you. This is important." Tyler continued to walk away. "It's about Andre," Chantal screamed.

"Go have a seat in the living room. I'll be with you shortly." Tyler walked back to the door. "What do you want, Chantal?"

"Please, I only need a few minutes. You need to hear this."

"Let her go," Tyler said reluctantly. "You have five minutes and that's being generous. Then I want you gone, or I'll have you thrown out."

"Fine." Chantal exhaled as the women stood in the foyer. "I know you saw the picture, but nothing happened between me and Andre."

"So what were doing in your lingerie?"

"I'll admit I did try to seduce him. When he came to visit Melanie I pulled out all the stops. But he rejected me," Chantal said putting her head down.

"Why should I believe you?"

"Why would I lie? Do you think I like standing here degrading myself by confessing that I pranced around half naked and I couldn't get Andre back in my bed?"

"So why are you here?" Tyler asked, not convinced with Chantal's admission.

"I'm trying to do the right thing for the first time in my life, and it's not because of you or Andre, but for my daughter. She loves her dad more than anything, and I know that if I continue to use the relationship he has with her to try to get him back, he'll end up hating me and distancing himself from her because he doesn't want to have anything to do with me. All my life I've been selfish, and I still am in a lot of ways, but Melanie shouldn't suffer anymore because of it. Melanie and I aren't a packaged deal. I've finally accepted that Andre doesn't want me, but he does want his daughter and I have to separate the two."

"This sounds very noble, but maybe you're just trying to score brownie points with Andre."

"Even if that was the case it wouldn't matter. After I made a fool of myself, Andre and I sat down and had a serious talk and he kept it extra crispy with me. This is hard for me to acknowledge, especially to you." Chantal swallowed hard before continuing. "He's truly in love with you. I thought it was a passing infatuation because you're some famous movie star, but I was wrong. You have his heart—something that I was never able to obtain. I just hope you know how lucky you are, because I pulled every trick in the book and I couldn't make him love me. So if you want him, he's yours. I believe my five minutes are up, so I won't keep you any longer," Chantal said, turning to walk away.

"Thank you," Tyler said sincerely.

"You welcome. Oh, and Tyler."

"Yes?"

"You better not hurt him or I'll be back." Chantal gave a slight grin and left. "Now all I have to make is one last stop and I'll finally have my life on the right track."

T-Roc sat in the dark drinking a glass of Remy Martin Louis XIII cognac. Marvin Gaye's greatest hits were playing in the back as he reflected on what had taken place in the last few days. Tyler had completely shut him out. She didn't want anything to do with him no matter how many times he begged for her forgiveness.

Once Deanna was locked up and realized the charges against her were serious, she decided to lift the mute button and started answering questions the police didn't even ask, specifically about T-Roc's involvement with her son. Deanna insinuated that he had something to do with both her son's death and Chrissie's. When they questioned T-Roc, he admitted that he hired Evan thinking he was a private investigator, but that was it. T-Roc got the impression they weren't convinced, but with no direct evidence linking him to any illegal wrong doing, it boiled down to an improvable hunch on the detectives' part. T-Roc was relieved that he wasn't facing any criminal charges, but enough of his secrets had been exposed and he'd lost Tyler forever.

"Who could that be?" T-Roc said out loud when he heard someone knocking on his front door. He wasn't expecting any company and actually didn't want any. Coming to the realization that with all the schemes he put into effect, and he still didn't get the girl was weighing hard on his psyche. "Chantal, what are you doing here?"

"Hello to you too. Can I come in?"

T-Roc took his hand off the door letting it close without saying a word, but Chantal still came in. "I see you're sitting in the dark. You've been drinking and you have depressing music playing. Those are all clues that something has you in a funk. Why don't you tell me what's wrong."

"Chantal, go home or go do something productive with yourself."

"Actually I did. I just came from visiting Tyler."

"What, to gloat that having sex with Andre made front page news?"

"Despite how it appeared, Andre and I didn't have sex and I wanted Tyler to know that."

"Come again?"

"You heard me. Yes, I did try to seduce him, but he turned me down. He's in love with Tyler and I wanted her to know that. It was the least I could do for all the trouble I've caused."

"Chantal, are you telling me you've developed a conscience?"

"What I'm saying is that life is too short to chase after a person who doesn't want you, especially when they're in love with someone else. You go through all sorts of ridiculous changes to win them over, and then you wake up and they still don't love you or want you. I rather get over it now while I'm still in my twenties and can find another man than be in my fifties, bitter because love has passed me by."

"You seem to be taking it all in stride."

"I am, because I already have another contender."

"So soon? Who's the lucky man?"

"You."

"Me?" T-Roc laughed, obviously surprised by what Chantal said.

"Why is that so funny? We've had great sex together in the past and we have a lot in common."

"Yeah a little too much. You're the only woman I know who is just as deceitful as me...maybe more. Not to say that I don't find it to be very charming, but I don't think I want to go to bed every night with one eye open."

"You need someone who will keep you on your toes, and you know I will. But betray you...never. You admitted that you were the one who paid for my bail and legal fees. That speaks volumes."

"I already explained to you why I did that."

"You gave me some song and dance about wanting me out to disrupt Andre and Tyler's relationship. I do not doubt you had an ulterior motive, but deep down I also believe it's because you care about me. And the last place you want me is behind bars."

T-Roc never gave serious thought to it, but hearing Chantal say it, he knew she was right. He did care about her. She was trifling and manipulative, but something about her was engaging. "Maybe I do care about you. That don't mean I want to have a serious relationship with you."

"You rather sit around waiting for Tyler? I hate to be the bearer of bad news, but you'll be waiting for a mighty long time. She's not the woman for you, T-Roc. As screwed up in the head as she is, the girl has morals and stuff. You know deep down she wants to do the right thing. A woman like that would drive you crazy because she would spend all her time trying to change you. With me, you don't have to worry about that. In fact, we can scheme together."

"I don't know what to do with you."

"I have an idea where you can start."

Chantal tossed her Cleopatra crocodile Judith Leiber clutch purse on the couch. She then unbuttoned her red silk blouse, exposing a lace bra with her impossibly perfect breasts inviting T-Roc in. She slowly unzipped her tuxedo styled pants, leaving on her metallic Miu Miu gold platform jeweled heels.

T-Roc salivated watching each curve jiggle just right as she sashayed closer to him. Chantal outlined his luscious lips with the tip of her tongue before their mouths fully met. T-Roc wrapped his arm around Chantal's waist and pulled her tightly against his chest. His hands glided up and down her silky skin, making his dick harder. A new level of lust was erupting and T-Roc laid Chantal down on the chinchilla rug, dying to ravage her body. Chantal ripped off his clothes sprinkling kisses on every inch of muscle on his chest. T-Roc then took Chantal's face and lifted it up and put his tongue down her throat. His hands massaged her skin, then rested firmly on her ass as he lifted her legs up before entering her.

"Is this what you wanted?" T-Roc asked, staring into Chantal's eyes.

"Yes, baby," Chantal moaned.

"You sure?"

"Yes, this dick is all I need. You feel so damn good, baby," Chantal purred.

"So do you." T-Roc's mind got lost as his manhood soaked in Chantal's warm juices. He licked each delicious breast taking in the sweet scent of her body. They explored each other's bodies for what seemed like forever until both reached their climax.

"Damn that shit felt good," T-Roc said rolling over on his back.

"That was better than good. I could wake up and go to sleep each night with that dick inside of me."

T-Roc sat up and leaned over, gazing at Chantal. Her honey blonde waves fanned the rug, her body glistened, and her lips were beyond kissable. Beauty was definitely her gift.

"Let's get married," T-Roc finally said, and all Chantal could do was smile. She had finally landed her a husband.

"**Mother, I'm glad you could come** over," Tyler said, opening the front door.

"But of course. I was happy you called. Especially when you told me my grandson was here."

"He actually already went to bed. We had a long and busy day."

"That's fine, I'll come back over tomorrow to see him," Maria said, having a seat on the couch.

"Can I get you something?"

"No, I'm fine."

Tyler sat down on the other couch.

"You're not going to have a drink—no champagne?" Maria inquired

"No."

"I'm surprised."

"I don't need to drink anymore," Tyler said with a renewed confidence in her voice.

"I couldn't agree with you more, but we all know that isn't going to make you stop."

"I'm sorry I didn't say that right. I won't be drinking anymore because I don't need it in order to deal with my disappointments."

"Impressive," Maria said sarcastically. "What brought that on?"

"Seeing my father again for the first time in over twenty years." Tyler witnessed the color drain from her mother's face and her body stiffen. "Is it botox that has your face frozen because you can't be at a lost for words. That's humanly impossible, but then, are you human, because what type of mother would keep her children from their father? Only a monster."

"Tyler, I can explain," her voice trembled

"I'm sure you can, but I don't want to hear it. Do you know what you did to me by ripping him out of my life? I spent all of my teenage years and the majority of my young adult life blaming myself for my father never coming back. Do you remember when I was fifteen and I asked why hasn't Daddy come back for me and

Ella, and you looked me in my eyes and said he didn't want me? No child should ever have to hear those words."

"He wasn't good enough for you and Ella."

"And you are? Lady, you are truly living in a fantasy world. That is our father. We deserved to have him in our lives."

"I did what I believed was the best for you and Ella. I wanted to protect you."

"From what?"

"He didn't have his life together. He was going to bring us down."

"No, you did that all on your own. How dare you play God with our lives? I'll never forget what you did."

"Tyler, baby, I love you. You have to believe me. All I ever wanted to do was provide you and your sister with a good life, a nice home, pretty clothes, treat you two like the little princesses' that you were. Your father would've never given you that."

"Maybe not, but he would've given us love, and there is no price tag on that. But our father is back, and this time you won't take him away from us."

"So now you want him to be a part of your life?"

"Yes, and if you want to be a part of my life and your grandson's, you better learn to accept that."

"Your point has been made, Tyler. You know that I want to be a part of your life and Christian's. So if accepting your father is a stipulation, then so be it."

"Good, because although I disagree with a lot of your decisions and I still don't approve of your relationship with William, you're my mother and I do love you." Tyler walked her mother to the door and gave her a hug good-bye.

"I love you so much, Tyler," Maria kissed her daughter on the cheek.

"I know."

Tyler went upstairs and ran herself a hot bubble bath, surrounding the Jacuzzi top with Jo Malone amber and sweet orange candles. The smell of velvety amber, hints of incense and musk were heightened in the seductive scent. She closed her eyes taking in the evocative aroma that engulfed her entire body with warmth.

Her mind drifted off to the last time she felt Andre inside of her and how his lovemaking was intoxicating. Tyler could no longer fight the urge. Her heart and body was yearning for Andre.

She opened her eyes, desperate to reach the nearest phone, and there he was. "Andre, how long have you been standing there?"

"For a few minutes. I hope you don't mind. You looked so beautiful I wanted to appreciate every moment."

"No, I don't mind. I was actually about to call you."

"Tyler, you have to believe me. Nothing happened between me and Chantal," Andre proclaimed, kneeling down next to the tub.

"I know. Chantal came to see me today."

"I told her not to bother you. She so damn hard headed."

"Don't be upset. I'm glad she came to see me. At first I wasn't, but once I heard what she had to say I was."

"Did she tell you how much I love you?"

"Surprisingly, Chantal told me that and a lot of other things that I needed to hear. There might be hope for her after all," Tyler giggled.

"I don't care about that. I just want to know if there is hope for *us*."

"You tell me."

"Baby, I want us to be together more than anything. I can't imagine my life without you in it. I want to share my whole world with you."

"You mean that?"

"With every bone in my body."

"Then tell me what happened."

"I did, and you said Chantal backed up everything I told you."

"I'm not talking about Chantal."

"You're referring to that article in the Los Angeles Times," Andre said, turning his face away.

"Yes. If you really want us to be together then you can't shut me out. I need to know what happened...no secrets."

"No secrets," he repeated as he began telling the story of what happened so many years ago.

"Back then, I was seventeen, wild and having fun. I would travel with my father sometimes when he would go overseas, and by then I was a celebrity in my own right with my own fans. The girl they're talking about in the article, Sheila, I was involved with her, but many parts of the article were completely fabricated. Sheila wasn't fifteen, she was eighteen, and she had traveled with me from the United States."

"Was she your girlfriend?" Tyler asked.

"I had so many women back then, but Sheila thought she was my girlfriend and I guess that's all that really mattered. We would have fun together and I enjoyed her company. That weekend was her birthday and she had never been overseas, so I invited her to come along as my gift to her. Some present that turned out to be."

"What went wrong?"

"I did. I gave Sheila some money to go shopping, and I was in the hotel lobby having some drinks when this sexy woman started flirting with me. I figured Sheila wouldn't be back for awhile so why not have sex with her? I took her upstairs to my hotel room and we became intimate."

"It had started pouring rain outside and Sheila got soaked and came back to the room to change, and she walked in on us having sex. She was hysterical and began crying and yelling. But instead of being sympathetic, I screamed on her and asked her why she didn't knock before coming in. She was humiliated and jumped on the girl trying to fight her, and then when I tried to get her off the girl, she scratched my face, neck, chest and back up. It was complete chaos in the room. The girl I was having sex with was terrified by Sheila's behavior and ran out of the room with just the bed sheet wrapped around her."

"Sheila began throwing everything and ransacked the room. And she kept on saying when she was doing all this was how much she loved me and that she was pregnant with my child. When she dropped that bomb, I became pissed and went ballistic. I told her she was a lying trick trying to trap me with a baby, but it wouldn't happen because I didn't give a damn about her and that she was just another piece of pussy to me. I told her to pack her shit and get out. I threw on my boxers to go find the other girl."

"Before I walked out, she looked at me and said, 'How can you do this to me? I just want to die right now'."

"I said, 'Go ahead, nobody is stopping you.' Those were the last words I said to her. I went up and down the hallway looking for the girl and I couldn't find her. I wasn't gone for more than five minutes, and when I went back in the room I saw Sheila's wet clothes on the floor leading towards the balcony." Andre put his head down and Tyler could hear him choking trying to hold back his tears.

"Andre, it's okay," she said reassuringly.

"No it's not. My body wouldn't go any further. My feet couldn't even touch the balcony because in my gut I knew she had jumped and it was entirely my fault. I may not have pushed her with my hands, but I did with my words. God forgive me." Andre said, breaking down in tears with his hands cupping his face.

Tyler didn't know what to say. There were no remarks she could use to take away the pain and guilt he was harboring.

Andre gathered his bearings and continued. "A few minutes later the cops came in and saw the scratches on my face and the trashed room, and when Sheila jumped she was naked, so they immediately arrested me assuming I was responsible for what happened, and technically I was responsible, just not physically, but emotionally."

"So how was the situation resolved?"

"It took a minute. I had to stay in jail for a few days. They couldn't find any ID on Sheila and she looked young so at first they claimed she was underage. They found the condom on the bed from when I had sex with the other girl and assumed I used it when I raped Sheila. It was a nightmare unraveling the mess I created. One thing that article was right about, once my father got wind of what happened he was able to hire the best lawyer and investigator to clear my name. The investigator found the woman Sheila had caught me with and she told the authorities that Sheila was the one who attacked us and trashed the room. And after the police investigated, they could tell by the way Sheila landed from the fall that she jumped and wasn't pushed."

"Thank goodness."

"Yeah, but I left there a changed person and not for the better. I blamed Sheila for turning my life upside down and was bitter and resentful towards women, especially after the autopsy was done and it revealed she wasn't even pregnant. I became even more of a womanizer. I was such a selfish man," Andre admitted, shaking his head in disappointment.

"Then when that article came out, although it was full of inaccuracies, it brought back all the memories I had suppressed. It made me think of the time Chantal slit her wrists and then when she hit you with the car. I had to admit that my egotistical behavior brought out the worst in women, and I was wrong for that. That's why I turned away from you, because I felt like a monster that didn't deserve you."

"Andre, look at me."

He turned to face Tyler as they gazed in each other's eyes.

"Would you ever do anything to hurt me like that?"

"I swear on everything that I love, no. Experiencing love for the first time with you has turned my life around. I'm a changed man."

"Then you do deserve me, because you're the only man I want to spend the rest of my life with."

Andre lifted Tyler out the bathtub and carried her to their bed. "Baby, I'm home and I'll never leave you again," he said before the two made love.

Chapter Eighteen

Stars Are Blind

"Baby, don't be nervous, you'll do fine," Tyler said as the lady finished touching up her makeup.

"But this is the Oprah Winfrey Show. She's the queen of all media and millions of people watch her show. What if I go on there and can't say a word?"

"Then I'll nudge your arm and speak for you until you get it together. We're a team. Together we can get through anything."

And that's what they did. Andre and Tyler sat down on the most sought after couch and shared their stories. For the first time Andre spoke publicly about what happened to Sheila that day in the hotel room. He gave every detail revealing his shame, accepting responsibility, and the valuable lesson he finally learned.

Tyler discussed her one time dependence on alcohol and turning to it to relieve pain she didn't want to face. She also revealed how being without her dad for so many years had left her with low self-esteem and feeling insecure. She declared that now she no longer needed alcohol or pills to take away the pain, but instead chose to discuss her issues and disappoints instead bottling them up.

Oprah and the audience were moved by both of their honesty and hoped that other men and women would learn from their growing pains.

"Girl, I can't believe Andre was on the 'Oprah Winfrey Show'," Shari said, shaking her head as she and Chantal sat in the living room watching the program.

"Yeah, that shit was good though," Chantal said, turning the power off on the remote as the show's credits rolled.

"It's amazing how shit can change in six months. You're living in Beverly Hills, married to T-Roc. Tyler and Andre are walking down the aisle tomorrow. Are you going to the wedding?"

"Hussy, shut up. But actually Tyler did send me an invitation, but T-Roc threw it in the trash."

"Why?"

"He doesn't want to admit it, but he still hung up on her. Or maybe his ego can't take that Andre won the so-called prize. But whatever it is, he'll get over it."

"Well, you look happy and he seems to be treating you good."

"No doubt. You can never call T-Roc cheap. He's very romantic and Melanie adores him. And guess what?"

"What?"

"I'm pregnant, with twins!"

"Chantal, are you serious?"

"Yep, and T-Roc is thrilled. This will be his first child, I mean children, we are having two."

"How far along are you, because you're not even showing?"

"You know I carried small with Melanie and I'm damn sure going to do the same with these two. You know my body is a commodity and the snap-back will still be in affect after I give birth."

"Bravo to you, bitch. You have done it. It looks as if we're both officially going from *Hooker to Housewife*. I'm so proud."

"What you mean 'us'?" Chantal was perplexed.

"You haven't noticed, but I've been keeping my hands hidden because I wanted to surprise you. Here, take a look." Shari extended her engagement finger and a monstrous, clear emerald-cut diamond decorated her finger. "Jalen proposed last night."

Chantal just stared for a few moments without uttering a sound.

"Chantal, say something."

"Didn't I call it? I knew your spaceship had landed. Girl, get over here and give me a hug." Shari scooted over to Chantal and the girls embraced, and then Chantal pushed her back. "You ain't pregnant are you?"

"Nope, I'm saving that for after the honeymoon."

The ladies did their signature pinky shake, gossiping and laughing for the rest of the day.

"Can I come in?" William asked, knocking on the half-open door to T-Roc's office.

"Of course, I always have time for my favorite director."

"Sorry to barge in but nobody was at the receptionist desk."

"Don't worry about it, it's Friday. I let everyone go home early."

"So how do you like having your headquarters and living full time in Beverly Hills now?"

"I'm enjoying it. The weather is great and New York is only a private jet ride away."

When William moved closer to T-Roc's desk he noticed he was holding a section of today's paper with the headline, *Wedding of the year.*

"I'm having a hard time letting go too," William said, catching T-Roc off guard.

T-Roc didn't understand what he meant until he looked down and realized he was still holding the paper that gave all the details about Tyler's and Andre's wedding. "I'm fine, really."

"Are you sure?"

"I guess I don't sound too convincing. William, you know Tyler almost better than anyone. I just want to know why?"

"Why what?"

"Why Tyler chose Andre. She could've had you, me, but she chose him. Why?"

"That is the same question I've asked myself many of times. And I've come back to the same answer. You can't decide who you fall in love with, it just happens. I wish I could stop loving Tyler but I can't. What I can do is move on with my life and wish her nothing but happiness. I advise you to do the same, and I don't mean going through the motions. Really focus on your new life."

"And I do have a lot to focus on. Chantal is pregnant. I'm going to be a father for the first time and she's having twins."

"Congratulations. That's wonderful news. Having those twins will be your biggest job and greatest accomplishment yet."

"I think so too."

"With two new babies coming and a movie that is bound to catapult you to the top, you have a lot to smile about."

"Have you come up with a title for the movie yet?"

"As a matter of fact I have."

"What is it?"

"The only title befitting... 'Superstar'."

"Tyler, you look amazing," Ella gushed as the stylist made a last minute alteration to her Christian Dior haute couture creation.

"I can't believe it's my wedding day. In less than an hour I will be Mrs. Andre Jackson." Tyler stared at her reflection in the full length mirror. Her life had come full circle. "Someone's at the door," Tyler said, startled by the knock.

"Calm down, I'll get," Ella said, patting Tyler's arm trying to soothe her nerves.

"But what if it's Andre? He can't see me in my dress yet."

"Then I won't let him in. But looking at the time, Andre should be at the altar waiting for you."

"I'm ready." Tyler touched her veil which looked like a confectionary of tulle.

"Daddy, come in," Ella said as she opened the door. "Maybe you can help Tyler to relax while I go take my position for the ceremony." Ella kissed her father on the cheek and left the room.

He stood looking at Tyler for a few seconds in complete silence. "You are simply breathtaking. A father couldn't have asked for a more beautiful daughter. I'm so proud of you." A tear slid down her father's face and Tyler wiped it away.

"Daddy, don't cry. You're supposed to be my rock as I have the breakdown." Tyler smiled and her whole face lit up.

"I know, but I never dreamed that I would be the one to walk you down the aisle on your wedding day. These last few months I feel as if I've been reborn, and that's because I have you and Ella back in my life."

"I feel the same way."

"Tyler, you look simply breathtaking. I'm so proud to have you as a daughter," Maria said, walking up from behind them. She then turned to look at her ex-husband who she hadn't seen in many years. "I hate to interrupt this father and daughter moment, but Carter, can I have a word with you?"

"Maria, I don't have time. This is Tyler's day and whatever you have to say to me can wait."

"It will only take a few minutes."

"Daddy, its fine. We have a few minutes to spare. I'll go check myself in the mirror one last time before my big moment." Tyler walked off leaving the former couple alone.

"What do you have to say, Maria?"

"I'm sorry."

"Sorry, for what? That I came back for my daughters?"

"No, that I kept them from you. Back then I truly believed I was doing what was best for my girls, but now I know I was doing what was best for me. You know how hard it is for me to admit my shortcomings, but I was wrong and I hope one day you can forgive me."

"I'll never get back all those years I lost with my girls. But I'm grateful that I'm still alive and have the opportunity to be a part of their lives. They are both remarkable young women. You did a great job raising them."

"I can't take credit for that. Honestly, Carter, both of them inherited your kind spirit, and I thank you for that."

Carter gave Maria a silent nod, letting her know that time truly heals all wounds and all was forgiven.

"Come on, Daddy, we have to go."

Maria gave Tyler a kiss and rushed off to her seat, and Tyler and her father embraced. "Now come walk me down this aisle."

Tyler and her father walked into the foyer of the Le Chateau Rose in Bel Air. The stunning private mansion was the perfect place for a fairytale wedding. A circular front courtyard with a fountain and 65' waterfall greeted you, and if that wasn't inviting enough, the magnificent ocean view and the original Baccarat crystal chandeliers from an 18th century chateau would cause even the most anti-marriage couple to hear wedding bells.

The music filled the room and the outstretched branches of one-hundred birch trees arched over the aisle as Tyler made her entrance with her father right by her side. There were three hundred and fifty attendees to witness the exchange of vows in the winter wonderland filled with 25,000 white roses, hydrangeas, and lilies of the valley.

When Tyler's father handed her to Andre, she became locked in his eyes, becoming spellbound. She could see their next fifty years flashing through his eyes; children, grandchildren, and growing old together.

The couple listened as the minister presiding over the ceremony read a scripture from the Bible. Tyler and Andre then exchanged vows before they were pronounced man and wife. Before the minister could say you may kiss the bride, the two lovebird's lips were interlocked.

Tyler Blake had taken the road less traveled and found her way. She had it all—love, eternal fulfillment, and was now a bonafide superstar!

The End

Joy King

About the Author

Joy King was born in Toledo, Ohio, and raised in California, Maryland, North Carolina and New Jersey. She is representing a new genre of young, hip sexy novels that take readers behind the velvet rope of the glamorous, but often shady entertainment industry, and street life in all its complexity.

Joy attended North Carolina Central University and Pace University, where she majored in journalism. Emerging onto the entertainment scene, Joy accepted an internship position, and immediately began to work her way up the ranks, at The Terrie Williams Agency. She worked hands-on with Johnnie Cochran, The Essence Awards, The Essence Music Festival, The NBA Players' Association, Moet & Chandon, and other entertainment executives and celebrities.

Following a new chapter in her life, Joy attended the Lee Strasburg Theater Institute before accepting a job as Director of Hip Hop Artist Relations at Click Radio, where she developed segments featuring the biggest names in hip hop. Joy pushed her department to new levels by creating an outlet that placed hip hop in the forefront of the cyber world.

Joy made her literary debut with Dirty Little Secrets, a novel that is loosely based on her life. A prolific writer, King also writes under the pseudonym Deja King and Katina King. Visit www.joykingonline.com to find out about her next novel.

Stackin'

Paper

a novel

by

Joy King

&

JoeJoe

Chapter One

A Killer Is Born

Philly, 1993

"Please, Daquan, don't hit me again!" the young mother screamed, covering her face in defense mode. She hurriedly pushed herself away from her predator, sliding her body on the cold hardwood floor.

"Bitch, get yo' ass back over here!" he barked, grabbing her matted black hair and dragging her into the kitchen. He reached for the hot skillet from the top of the oven, and you could hear the oil popping underneath the fried chicken his wife had been cooking right before he came home. "Didn't I tell you to have my food ready on the table when I came home?"

"I… I… I was almost finished, but you came home early," Teresa stuttered, "Ouch!" she yelled as her neck damn near snapped when Daquan gripped her hair even tighter.

"I don't want to hear your fuckin' excuses. That's what yo' problem is. You so damn hard headed and neva want to listen. But like they say, a hard head make fo' a soft ass. You gon' learn to listen to me."

"Please, please, Daquan, don't do this! Let me finish frying your chicken and I'll never do this again. Your food will be ready and on the table everyday on time. I promise!"

"I'm tired of hearing your damn excuses."

"Bang!" was all you heard as the hot skillet came crashing down on Teresa's head. The hot oil splashed up in the air, and if

Daquan hadn't moved forward and turned his head, his face would've been saturated with the grease.

But Teresa wasn't so lucky, as the burning oil grazed her hands, as they were protecting her face and part of her thigh.

After belting out in pain from the grease, she then noticed blood trickling down from the open gash on the side of her forehead. But it didn't stop there. Daquan then put the skillet down and began kicking Teresa in her ribs and back like she was a diseased infected dog that had just bitten him.

"Yo', Pops, leave moms alone! Why you always got to do this? It ain't never no peace when you come in this house." Genesis stood in the kitchen entrance with his fists clenched and panting like a bull. He had grown sick and tired of watching his father beat his mother down almost every single day. At the age of eleven he had seen his mother receive more ass whippings than hugs or any indication of love.

"Boy, who the fuck you talkin' to? You betta get yo' ass back in your room and stay the hell outta of grown people's business."

"Genesis, listen to your father. I'll be alright. Now go back to your room," his mother pleaded.

Genesis just stood there unable to move, watching his mother and feeling helpless. The blood was now covering her white nightgown and she was covering her midsection, obviously in pain trying to protect the baby that was growing inside of her. He was in a trance, not knowing what to do to make the madness stop. But he was quickly brought back to reality when he felt his jaw almost crack from the punch his father landed on the side of his face.

"I ain't gon' tell you again. Get yo' ass back in your room! And don't come out until I tell you to! Now go!" Daquan didn't even wait to let his only son go back to his room. He immediately went over to Teresa and picked up where he left off, punishing her body with punches and kicks. He seemed oblivious to the fact that not only was he killing her, but also he was killing his unborn child right before his son's eyes.

A tear streamed down Genesis's face as he tried to reflect on one happy time he had with his dad, but he went blank. There were no happy times. From the first moment he could remember, his dad was a monster.

All Genesis remembered starting from the age of three was the constant beat downs his mother endured for no reason. If his dad's clothes weren't ironed just right, then a blow to the face. If the volume of the television was too loud, then a jab here. And, God forbid, if the small, two-bedroom apartment in the drug-infested building they lived in wasn't spotless, a nuclear bomb would explode in the form of Daquan. But the crazy part was, no matter how clean their apartment was or how good the food was cooked and his clothes being ironed just right, it was never good enough. Daquan would bust in the door, drunk or high, full of anger, ready to take out all his frustration out on his wife. The dead end jobs, being broke, living in the drug infested and violent prone city of Philadelphia had turned the already troubled man into poison to his whole family.

"Daddy, leave my mom alone," Genesis said in a calm, unemotional tone. Daquan kept striking Teresa as if he didn't hear his son. "I'm not gonna to tell you again. Leave my mom alone." This time Daquan heard his son's warning but seemed unfazed.

"I guess that swollen jaw wasn't enough for you. You dying to get that ass beat." Daquan looked down at a now black and blue Teresa who seemed to be about to take her last breath. "You keep yo' ass right here, while I teach our son a lesson." Teresa reached her hand out with the little strength she had left trying to save her son. But she quickly realized it was too late. The sins of the parents had now falling upon their child.

"Get away from my mother. I want you to leave and don't ever come back."

Daquan was so caught up in the lashing he had been putting on his wife that he didn't even notice Genesis retrieving the gun he left on the kitchen counter until he had it raised and pointed in his direction. "Lil' fuck, you un lost yo' damn mind! You gon' make me beat you with the tip of my gun."

Daquan reached his hand out to grab the gun out of Genesis's hand, and when he moved his leg forward, it would be the last step he'd ever take in his life. The single shot fired ripped through Daquan's heart and he collapsed on the kitchen floor, dying instantly.

Genesis was frozen and his mother began crying hysterically. "Oh dear God!" Teresa moaned, trying to gasp for air. "Oh, Genesis baby, what have you done?" She stared at Daquan, who laid face up with his eyes wide open in shock. He died not believing until it was too late that his own son would be the one to take him out this world.

It wasn't until they heard the pounding on the front door that Genesis snapped back to the severity of the situation at hand.

"Is everything alright in there?" they heard the older lady from across the hall ask.

Genesis walked to the door still gripping the .380-caliber semi-automatic. He opened the door and said in a serene voice, "No, Ms. Johnson, everything is *not* alright. I just killed my father."

■■■■■■

Two months later, Teresa cried as she watched her son being

taking away to spend a minimum of two years in a juvenile facility in Pemberton, New Jersey.

Although it was obvious by the bruises on both Teresa and Genesis that he acted in self defense, the judge felt that the young boy having to live with the guilt of murdering his own father wasn't punishment enough. He concluded that if Genesis didn't get a hard wake up call, he would be headed on a path of self destruction. He first ordered him to stay at the juvenile facility until he was eighteen. But after pleas from his mother, neighbors and his teacher, who testified that Genesis had the ability to accomplish whatever he wanted in life because of how smart and gifted he was, the judge reduced it to two years, but only if he demonstrated excellent behavior during his time there. Those two years turned into four and four turned into seven. At the age of eighteen when Genesis was finally released he was no longer a young boy, he was now a criminal minded man.

Stackin' Paper
In Stores
Now!!

Deja King

Who brought you the Bitch Series
introduces her gritty new Trilogy...

Trife Life

2

Lavish

Coming 2009

A KING PRODUCTION PRESENTS

In Stores Now

Superstar
by Joy King

Dirty Little Secrets
by Joy King

Hooker to Housewife
by Joy King

Bitch
by Deja King

Bitch Reloaded
by Deja King

The Bitch Is Back
by Deja King

Ride Wit' Me
by Katina King

And

Stackin' Paper
by Joy King & JoeJoe

Coming Soon...

Stackin' Paper II: Genesis's Payback
by Joy King & JoeJoe

And

Trife Life 2 Lavish
by Deja King

Read All Of
A King Productions
#1 Bestsellers

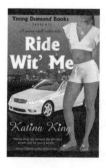

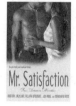

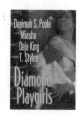

A King Production
Order Form

A King Production
P.O. Box 912
Collierville, TN 38027
www.myspace.com/joyking

Name: _____
Address: _____
City/State: _____
Zip: _____

QUANTITY	TITLES	PRICE EACH	TOTAL
____	Bitch	$15.00	_____
____	Bitch Reloaded	$15.00	_____
____	The Bitch Is Back	$15.00	_____
____	Dirty Little Secrets	$14.95	_____
____	Hooker to Housewife	$13.95	_____
____	Superstar	$15.00	_____
____	Ride Wit' Me	$12.00	_____
____	Stackin' Paper	$15.00	_____
____	Mr. Satisfaction	$13.95	_____
____	These Are My Confessions	$13.95	_____
____	Diamond Playgirls	$15.00	_____

Shipping/Handling (Via U.S. Media Mail) $3.95 1-2 Books, $5.95 3-4 Books add $1.95 for ea. Additional book

Total $_____

FORMS OF ACCEPTED PAYMENTS:
Certified or government issued checks and money Orders, all mail in orders take 5-7 Business days to be delivered.